A VALENTINE FOR VALERIE

LOVE WILL OUT, BOOK #6

D.E. HAGGERTY

Copyright © 2022 D.E. Haggerty

All rights reserved.

D.E. Haggerty asserts the moral right to be identified as the author of this work.

ISBN: 9798792461253

A Valentine for Valerie is a work of fiction. The names, characters, places, and incidents portrayed in it are the product of the author's imagination. Any resemblance to actual persons, living or dead, events or locations is entirely coincidental.

All rights reserved. No part of this publication may be reproduced, stored in a retrieval system, or transmitted, in any form or by any means, electronic, mechanical, photocopying, recording or otherwise, without the prior permission of the author.

Also by D.E. Haggerty

A Hero for Hailey

A Protector for Phoebe

A Soldier for Suzie

A Fox for Faith

A Christmas for Chrissie

Dutch Treat

Double Dutch

Dutch Courage

Dutch Online

About Face

At Arm's Length

Hands Off

Knee Deep

Molly's Misadventures

The Billionaire Option

Buried Appearances

Searching for Gertrude

To Sergeant Lewis
Farewell, my brother

Chapter 1

We're not socks, but I think we'd make a great pair.

"We need to talk, Valerie." I scowl at Barney's declaration. I have spent my entire life avoiding having the 'talk' with a man. Barney Lewis is not going to ruin my streak.

He may be one sexy middle-aged man – my hands itch to run through the soft texture of his black hair once again and his ever present five o'clock shadow gives my body all kinds of ideas of how his stubble will feel scratching certain areas of my delicate skin – but his handsome appearance doesn't give him the right to boss me around.

Especially not when we're at a wedding. A surprise wedding on Christmas day no less. Barney's friend, Wally, proposed to his girlfriend, Chrissie, this morning, and then when they arrived at McGraw's Pub to celebrate Christmas with everyone, he surprised her with a wedding. Naturally, Chrissie freaked out, but we got her down the aisle eventually.

Welp. Best get this stupid 'talk' over with, so I can get back to enjoying the party. I indicate the hallway leading to the restrooms. When he lifts his chin in agreement, I square my shoulders and march to the hallway as if I'm not dreading this stupid conversation.

Barney doesn't immediately follow me. Of course not. He doesn't want anyone to know what we've been up to after all. He made those thoughts perfectly clear when he ran away from me on Saturday evening after kissing the daylights out of me.

I reach the hallway and lean against the wall to

wait. I cross my arms over my chest and tap my toe as I become impatient – or more impatient, I should say. I don't want to be in the hallway having some conversation with Barney I don't want to have. I want to be in the pub celebrating my friend getting married.

Barney appears at the mouth of the hallway and grabs my hand before leading me to the office. His friend, Max, owns McGraw's Pub. Max is engaged to my friend, Faith, which is how I ended up in this bar in the first place.

"We need to talk," he repeats once we're behind the locked door in the office.

I stand in the middle of the room and place my hands on my hips. "So you said." I raise an eyebrow and wait for him to speak.

He bites his lip and my mind flashes back to when we made out in this very office a few days ago. It was me biting his lip then. His responding growl made me want to throw him down on the floor and have my way with him. Unfortunately, the man made a break for it before I got the chance.

When Barney doesn't speak, I throw my hands in the air. "Well? Are you going to say actual words or are you going to stand there and stare at me?"

"We need to talk."

"Dude, you said those words three times already. Get to saying whatever you've got to say so we can get this over with and get back to the wedding reception."

"It's about us."

"There is no us," I interrupt to say.

I don't do relationships. I may love romance – and I do seriously love romance – but I know better than to expect it for myself. It's an illusion after all. Once there's a ring on someone's finger, they change and anything resembling love and romance flies out the window.

He clears his throat. "Exactly."

"Good. We agree. Are we done here? I want to get my drink on and celebrate with Chrissie and my friends."

My friends. I smile at those words. For such a long time, my only friend was Faith. And when Faith left Saint Louis with her son Ollie to live in Milwaukee, my circle of friends was reduced to zero. I can't be mad at Faith for abandoning me, though, not when she found the love of her life in Max. He proposed to her on Thanksgiving and now they're planning a Valentine's Day wedding. I am beyond happy for her.

When I had to leave my job in Saint Louis, I decided to follow Faith to Milwaukee. It's working out well thus far. Faith's crazy group of friends didn't hesitate to include me. Now, I feel more at home here than I ever did in Saint Louis despite growing up and living there my entire life.

"Don't drink too much," Barney orders.

"No man tells me what to do." I march to the door to escape before this conversation becomes awkward – or more awkward, I should say.

Barney clamps a hand down on my shoulder to thwart my escape. I whirl around on him. "What is it now?"

"I don't want you to be mad at me."

"Dude, you could give a woman whiplash. You don't want a relationship with me? Fine. I completely and totally understand. But don't pretend to care how I feel."

He growls. "I do care how you feel. You're my fr—" He clears his throat. "You're my brother's woman's friend."

His brother's woman's friend? I roll my eyes. He can't even say we're friends? Geez. Thanks for nothing, pal.

"I'm not mad. I'm annoyed because I don't want to be here."

Pain flashes in his eyes before he blinks, and it's gone. Did I say the guy could give a gal whiplash? I was wrong. He's going to give me a migraine with the way he runs hot and cold.

I admit it was fun chasing after the guy for the past month. I do love a good chase. And the way he panicked every time I got close made it all the more fun. But since he's made it perfectly clear he's not up for a roll in the hay with me, I'm done chasing. I don't chase men who don't want to be chased. I'm not a predator.

I inhale a deep breath and straighten my shoulders. I guess I have to be the adult here. And I do hate being the adult. "I understand. You're not interested. I'm a big girl. I can handle it."

He rakes a hand through his hair. "It's not...I'm not..."

I pat his shoulder. "It's fine. Our lives are intertwined because of our friends. We can be casual acquaintances."

I march to the door and fling it open to find Faith and her gang of friends – Suzie, Phoebe, and Hailey – waiting on me. Well, not all of the gang.

"Where's Chrissie?" I ask.

"She left for her honeymoon," Faith answers.

"Honeymoon? Wally arranged a surprise wedding and a honeymoon? He literally proposed this morning. He must have been awful sure of himself."

Suzie snorts. "Have you met Wally? The super-secret spy is very sure of himself."

"Is he a super-secret spy if you know about it?"

We all think Wally is some type of super-spy after what happened with Chrissie. I don't know much about it, but apparently, she was in danger from an ex. Wally gathered his former military buddies – including Barney – together and they managed to catch the guy. Since Chrissie is a badass herself, I can only imagine how scary the situation was.

Lexi saunters into the hallway but stops when she notices all of us standing there. Lexi is a friend of Chrissie's who showed up at the last minute to attend the wedding. "What's going on?"

Faith raises her eyebrow at me. "Exactly what I want to know."

"Yeah, Valerie." Suzie scans my body. "What were you doing locked up with Barney in the office?"

Hailey smiles and rubs her hands together. "They were obviously not getting down and dirty, which means I'm still in the running to win this bet."

Faith frowns. "Christmas day isn't over yet."

I widen my eyes to feign innocence. Ha! I haven't been innocent in a long ass time. "What are you talking about?"

I know exactly what they're talking about. Barney and his friends bet on everything under the sun. Somehow the women got involved and now they throw out bets like crazy. Everyone's currently betting on when Barney and I will finally 'get together'. Considering the 'talk' Barney just subjected me to, Faith is definitely losing this bet.

Speaking of Barney, where is he? He's not in the office listening to us talk, is he? I glance over my shoulder, but he's not there. What the heck?

"If you're searching for Barney, he's gone," Hailey says. "My uncles can disappear into thin air."

Hailey considers Barney and his friends her uncles since they helped raise her after her mom took off when she was young. In addition to Barney, the 'uncles' include Wally, Sid, and Lenny. All of them, plus Hailey's dad, Max, know each other from their military days. The brothers are now handsome middle-aged men who haven't let age slow them down one bit. Faith definitely hit the lottery when she walked into McGraw's Pub searching for a job.

"Speaking of Barney," Faith begins.

I hold up a hand to stop her. "Nope. I'm not talking about it."

Her shoulders slump. "Okay."

Suzie wrinkles her nose. "Okay? No, it's not okay. I veto. I want to hear about it. Whatever it is."

"I'm guessing it has something to do with Barney scrambling after Valerie on Saturday night after his 'date' showed up." Hailey stares at me as if she's waiting for me to contradict her.

She can keep waiting. I know Faith and her friends get all up in each other's business, but I'm not telling them what happened. Not because I'm embarrassed. I'm not. Barney was the one who was embarrassed when Wally pranked him with a male date. I don't know why. Being gay is nothing to be ashamed of.

But Barney's embarrassment was to my advantage when he shoved me up against the wall and told me he was going to prove he's not into men. It was one of the sexiest moments of my life. Unfortunately, the sexy ended there. After kissing all the common sense out of me, he ripped his mouth from mine and sauntered off without a word spoken.

Time for a diversion, because I'm not telling anyone what happened on Saturday night. I clap my hands. "Who's ready to learn who the real karaoke queen is?"

Suzie's hand shoots into the air. "It's me."

I wink at her. "I guess it's time for you to prove it."

Chapter 2

My boyfriend and I met on the internet. My mother asked him what line he used on me and my boyfriend replied, "I just used a modem."

"Good morning," I greet Faith as she trudges past my desk.

"Good morning," she mumbles.

Wait for it. One, two, three.

Faith rocks to a halt before whirling around to stare at me. "Val? What are you doing here?"

My brow wrinkles as I scan the interior of the law firm offices and feign confusion. "I think I'm working?"

"But you don't live in Milwaukee. You live in Saint Louis. I thought you were going back home on the first of the year."

Nope. I've moved to Milwaukee, but she doesn't exactly know about it because someone's been keeping a secret from her friend. A big fat secret in fact. A secret called 'I can't go back to Saint Louis'. I mean, I can. I haven't been banned or kicked out or banished or anything. But I did lose my job there. Lose as in got fired and kicked out on my ass despite working there for nearly twenty years. The jerks.

But I haven't told Faith about the incident. She's had enough going on in her life with planning for a wedding and moving into Max's apartment with her son without me adding all of my problems.

I shrug. "I thought I'd give Milwaukee a try. It seems to agree with you."

She smiles. "Yeah, it does. When did you—"

My intercom beeps and interrupts whatever Faith was going to say. "Ms. Cook, can you join me, please?"

"Right away," I say before grabbing a pen and paper and standing.

Before I can escape, Faith stops me. "You. Me. Lunch. Today."

I nod before rushing into the office behind me. I can't avoid her now that we're working for the same law firm. To be honest, I don't want to avoid her. Do I want to tell her what happened in Saint Louis? Not even a little bit. But I don't need to avoid her to keep my secret.

I'm not surprised Faith and I ended up working at the same law firm again. After all, it's how we met. We worked for the same firm in Saint Louis where I was a legal secretary and Faith a paralegal. But I didn't know Faith worked at this law firm in Milwaukee when I took the job. I only realized it a few seconds ago when I saw her sauntering past me.

It will be nice working at the same firm with Faith again. Being a legal secretary isn't exactly the most exciting job in the universe – lawyers expect you to dress and act like a responsible adult all the time and adulting isn't exactly fun – but having my friend around will liven things up.

The morning passes in a whirl. I thought starting my new job in the downtime between Christmas and New Year's Day would give me a chance to adjust to my position before the new year got rolling. Guess I was wrong.

The attorney for whom I work, Mr. Davenport, keeps me busy all morning. I have a feeling I'm going to be working a ton of overtime with him as a boss. Fine by me. I don't exactly have a husband or family to go home to after all.

Faith arrives in front of my desk at exactly twelve o'clock. "Grab your coat."

She looks like she's ready to do battle. I don't know why. I'm not going to fight her on going out for lunch.

After the morning I've had, I'm ready for a break and some sustenance. My stomach rumbles in agreement.

We don't speak as we exit the building. Faith leads me to a sandwich shop down the street from the office building. We find a booth in the back before she orders me to, "Spill."

I shrug. "There's not much to say. Saint Louis was boring without you and Ollie there."

I'm not lying. Maybe I should be embarrassed to say it, but Faith and Ollie were pretty much my only friends in the city. I certainly don't have any contact with my family. I haven't spoken to my mom since the day I walked out when I was seventeen. There's not much to say when your mom accuses you of trying to seduce your stepfather.

Besides my mom, I don't have any relatives. I never knew who my dad was, and my mom's family threw her out when she got pregnant with me or so claims my mom. I think it probably had more to do with mom's substance abuse problems. Trust me. Being around an addict is no picnic.

Faith clutches my hand. "I'm sorry. I know I took off without telling you. I should have told you what was happening."

"You don't have to tell me, but I assume everything is okay now?"

When she snuck off in the middle of the night, leaving most of her furniture and possessions behind, I knew something was wrong. I never pushed her on it, though. Not even when she cancelled her phone and wouldn't provide me with a new phone number. She insisted the only way we could communicate was via Facebook messenger.

I didn't complain. After all, she didn't cut me off completely. And I wasn't going to cause any problems for her. Not when I didn't know what kind of trouble she was in.

"Everything's fine. Max and his military brothers took care of it."

At the word 'brothers', my body warms thinking about one particular brother. Barney. Oh boy, does the man know how to use his lips and tongue. I can't help but wonder how his tongue would feel on other parts of my body. I shove those fantasies aside. I'll revisit them later when I'm in bed alone.

Faith clears her throat. "It was Ollie. He got in trouble," she begins and then goes on to tell me how her son antagonized one of the gangs in Saint Louis causing them to flee the city until things settled down. And when they didn't settle down, Max charged in and saved the day.

"You're lucky to have Max."

Her smile lights up the room. Faith is pretty with her long brown hair and dark eyes, but when she smiles, she's beautiful.

She squeezes my hand. "You could be lucky, too. Barney seems smitten with you."

I giggle. "Smitten. How old are you again?"

She sticks her tongue out at me. "We're the same age. Forty-five."

For some reason, she thinks Barney and I would make a good match. I have no idea why. She knows I don't do relationships. It doesn't matter what she thinks. I'm not talking about Barney with her. I return to our earlier topic of conversation.

"Anyway, Saint Louis was boring and after I came here and saw how great your life is, I thought I'd give Milwaukee a try."

Her eyes light up with excitement. "Then, you're staying for good?"

"I am."

"Yeah! I've missed you."

Her words warm me from the inside out. With all her new friends here, I worried she'd forget all about me. I'm glad she hasn't. "I've missed you, too. And Ollie. Is your boy ever going to stop growing?"

"I can't believe he's sixteen and driving. How am I

old enough to have a son who can drive?"

"This is how it works. First, you have unprotected sex." I waggle my eyebrows. "Then, the sperm—"

Faith waves her hands while yelling, "Stop! I don't need a sex education lesson."

I shrug. "If you're sure…"

"You're as bad as Suzie."

If she's trying to upset me, it isn't going to work. Suzie's awesome. Her crazy matches mine.

"You didn't move here for Barney?"

Crap. I thought I'd successfully maneuvered away from the topic of Barney and Valerie.

"Barney? Have you ever seen me do anything for a man?"

I'm not exaggerating. I do not bend my will for anyone and certainly not a man.

"Sorry. Sorry. I forgot who I was talking to." She leans close. "You have to admit, though, Barney is one sexy man."

He most certainly is. His tall body is packed full of lean muscles. Muscles I wouldn't mind running my hands and mouth all over. He's also a complete goofball who tells dirty jokes and pulls pranks on people. If I did do relationships, he'd be my number one choice. Good thing I don't, though, since Barney's made it perfectly clear he's not interested.

I ignore how his rejection causes my stomach to ache. I don't care what Barney thinks, I remind myself. My stomach obviously doesn't believe me as the ache deepens.

"Don't let your fiancé hear you call another man sexy," I chide Faith.

She rolls her eyes. "Max knows I would never cheat on him."

"I'm happy for you. After Silas, I thought you might give up on men."

Silas is Faith's ex-husband and Ollie's biological father. He's also a total and complete waste of space. While Faith worked her butt off to keep a roof over her and Ollie's heads and food on their table, Silas goofed off and cheated on her with anything with tits. Slimeball.

She raises an eyebrow. "Like you've given up on men?"

I scratch my head. "I'm confused. Didn't you accuse me of moving to Milwaukee for a man less than two minutes ago?"

She blows out a puff of air. "I suck at this 'trying to trick my friend into giving a relationship a go' thing."

I bark out a laugh. "Maybe you should have kept that information to yourself."

She waves away my concern. "You already had me figured out anyway."

True. Faith isn't one for subterfuge. Plus, we've been friends long enough for me to read her like a book.

"Tell me everything about the firm. Do you like it there? Who are the lawyers I need to stay away from?"

We may be in the twenty-first century, but some men haven't gotten with the program yet. They think it's okay to pinch a woman's butt or corner her in the copy room. Faith and I learned a long time ago to share information to prevent one of us from getting caught in a bad situation.

"Well…" she begins, and I eat my sandwich as she fills me in on all the gossip at the law firm.

Chapter 3

Did you hear about the porcupine who was near-sighted?
He fell in love with a pincushion.

"Knock! Knock!" Suzie shouts while pounding on my door on Friday night.

I march to the door and fling it open to find Suzie, Faith, Hailey, and Phoebe standing in the hallway.

"What is everyone doing here?" I ask. "Did I forget inviting you over?"

"We're not staying," Suzie says. "It's girls' night out and you'll be joining us."

Phoebe groans. "You said we're going to dinner. Baby Rossi's hungry." She rubs her baby bump.

Hailey rolls her eyes. "Baby Rossi's always hungry. Trust me. I know."

Hailey and Phoebe work together at the PI firm Hailey and Suzie started. It's called *You Cheat, We Eat.* The name cracks me up every time I hear it. Suzie doesn't work there anymore, though. She's too busy with her microbrewery since her husband, Grayson, stepped in and taught her how to market the business. Apparently, the former soldier is some kind of marketing guru.

Chrissie and Phoebe's husband, Ryker, work at the PI firm, too. Chrissie is the office manager while Ryker's a badass bounty hunter. In fact, Ryker and Phoebe met when Phoebe's husband hired him to find Phoebe. I don't know the whole story, but I admit I'm intrigued.

"Don't worry. We'll eat. Baby Grayson is hungry, too." Suzie points to her baby bump.

"How is it her baby bump is cute, but I look like I swallowed a basketball," Phoebe whines.

"Maybe because my husband is normal sized and yours is the size of a Yeti." Suzie mouths to me, *and hairy like one, too.*

Faith claps her hands. "Can we get back on topic now?"

Hailey crosses her arms over her chest. "What topic?" Good question.

"Duh. Girls' night out to celebrate Val moving to Milwaukee on a permanent basis. Grab your coat, Val."

Phoebe holds up her hand. "Can I use your bathroom first? Baby Rossi needs to pee."

I wave toward the hallway where the half bath is. "Go for it."

She rushes inside with Suzie hot on her heels. "You had to say pee, didn't you? Now I need to go."

Hailey frowns as she watches the two pregnant women rush to the bathroom. "I'm not sure about this having kids thing. Maybe I'll settle for being an aunt. After all, Suzie wants six kids."

"Six kids?" Gulp. "Her poor lady bits." I shiver. Thank goodness those days are over for me. Although, since they never got started, I'm thinking 'over' isn't the correct terminology.

"I'm more worried about Grayson. Can you imagine if their children are as crazy as her? Her husband will be surrounded," Hailey says, and I scowl.

What's wrong with being crazy? Life is freaking hard. A bit of crazy can help to ease the pain.

Faith throws her arm around me. "Personally, I enjoy a bit of crazy in my life."

"I could eat a horse," Phoebe says as she returns to the living room. Her stomach grumbles in agreement.

Hailey raises an eyebrow. "This from the woman who survived on rabbit food when she first arrived."

"Rabbit? I don't eat rabbit," Suzie says as she joins us. "Who wants rabbit?" She scrunches her nose at Phoebe. "Are you having weird cravings?"

"All right. Time for this show to get on the road." I herd everyone out the door and out of the apartment building into the parking lot where we pile into Hailey's SUV before driving to McGraw's Pub.

Since Hailey's dad owns the pub, she and her friends hang out here with her Pops all the time. Everyone calls Hailey's dad Pops. I call him Max. I can't call him Pops. It's too weird. He's not my dad after all.

McGraw's Pub is also where Barney and the rest of the former Army brothers can be found most evenings. Normally, I'd be excited at the prospect of a chance to be near Barney. Not anymore. I've learned my lesson. He's not interested. And I'm not one of those desperate women who chase after a man who isn't interested. A reluctant man? I'll chase after him all day and night. A man who has told me 'no' in no uncertain terms? I'm done chasing him.

Hailey arrives at the entrance and flings the door open to shout, "Honey, I'm home."

"Hey, baby cakes." Max smiles at his daughter before his gaze finds his fiancée and warms. "Hey, spitfire."

"Be right back," Faith says before rushing behind the bar.

"Ugh," Phoebe groans. "I swear they make out to torture me."

Suzie snorts. "Yeah, right."

"They're in love. I think it's awesome." Hailey isn't teasing Phoebe. She appears genuinely happy for her dad.

"It's your Pops. Aren't you bothered by how his tongue is down Faith's throat?" Phoebe asks Hailey.

"Nope."

"Please, be my ally here," Phoebe pleads with me.

"Sorry. Not sorry. Max is a stone-cold fox. I'd let

him stick his tongue down my throat any day."

I hear a growl behind me and whirl around to find Barney glaring at me. I roll my eyes. "Don't worry. I would never make a move on Faith's man. Or any engaged or married man for that matter."

He grunts before trudging past us to join Sid and Lenny at their table. It's a corner booth where the brothers spend their time playing poker and ragging on each other.

Suzie stares after him with her mouth gaping open. "Did Uncle Barney seriously walk past us without telling a dirty joke? Do you think he's sick? Should we call the doctor?"

Hailey giggles. "Barney's sick alright. Heartsick."

I am not listening to this. Hailey is trying to force Barney and me together because if we 'get together' on New Year's Eve, she wins the bet. She might as well kiss her money goodbye now. There's no way Barney and I are ever getting together.

I thread my arm through Phoebe's. "I'm hungry. Can we please get some food now?"

Phoebe and I find a table across the room from Barney with Hailey and Suzie. Faith joins us a few minutes later. Her face is flushed, and her hair is a mess.

"Sorry."

I wave away her apology. "No need to apologize."

Phoebe slaps my hand out of the air. "Speak for yourself. Someone needs to apologize for making me witness my honorary father make out with a woman."

"Not any woman, my fiancée," Max says as he arrives. He palms Faith's neck and leans down to kiss her again.

Phoebe covers her eyes with her hands. "They're doing it again!"

Hailey snorts. "When are you going to learn? You're making it worse for yourself."

Max comes up for air to ask, "What can I get you ladies to drink?"

"Baby Rossi wants the biggest hamburger you can make and a plate of fries."

"Baby Rossi? Not Phoebe?"

Phoebe elbows me. "No guilt tripping the pregnant lady. It's in the rule book."

"It is?" Suzie huffs. "Why didn't I know this? I'm pregnant, too," she announces as if we can't see she's pregnant.

"We also need a round of tequila shots," Hailey orders.

Her dad raises an eyebrow in response. "Tequila shots?"

"Yep. I've been tasked with discovering why Val quit her job and moved to Milwaukee all of a sudden."

"Psst. You're not supposed to tell Val you're going to get her drunk and make her spill her secrets," Suzie whisper-shouts.

Hailey shrugs. "It's all part of my plan." She narrows her eyes on me. "The pressure to cough up the truth starts now."

"Maybe I quit because I fell in love with my boss and he didn't return my feelings."

"Beep!" Faith shouts. "Your boss has the biggest beer belly in existence and a combover to boot. If you fell in love with him, I'm Cinderella."

"What if the law firm is downsizing and I got made redundant because I'd been there the longest?"

Faith rolls her eyes. "Sell it to someone who's buying."

"Maybe I missed Faith and Ollie."

"Oh!" Phoebe thrusts her hand into the air. "I know this one. You wouldn't have made up two elaborate lies first."

Max arrives with a bottle of tequila and three shot glasses. "Have fun, ladies."

I gulp. Tequila and I are not good friends. The

smell of it literally makes me gag. I blame the time in college when I bet I could drink my roommate's boyfriend under the table. He and my roommate were always getting busy in the room. I'm all for people getting as much sex as possible but not when I share a room with them. I'm not a voyeur.

I won the bet, but I spent two days with the worst hangover of my life, which is saying something since this girl's vocabulary doesn't include the word 'no' when asked if she wants another drink. But tequila? I don't touch the stuff when I'm sober.

I glare at Faith. "You know how much I hate tequila."

"And you know how much I hate secrets."

I cock an eyebrow. Isn't she the one who kept a secret from me for the past year?

Her cheeks darken. "And I was wrong. I should have told you what happened."

"What's going on?" Suzie asks as her gaze ping-pongs between us. "Are they telepathically communicating?" She rubs her hands together. "Can you teach me?"

Hailey bops her on the nose. "Telepathy doesn't exist."

"How do you know? I'll ask Chrissie when she's back from her honeymoon. She'll know."

"I just want to know you're safe," Faith says.

I blow out a breath of air. "Geez. If you're going to start with the guilt trip, I'll tell you."

"Whoa! Wait. Are we not going to try to drink each other under the table?" Hailey looks like someone took her fun away.

"You don't need me to drink tequila."

"Yes, I do. Aiden gets weird about me doing shots when he's not around. He acts like I can't take care of myself."

Her husband, Aiden, is a police detective. From

A Valentine for Valerie

what I've seen, he is a bit of a worrywart. Considering Hailey's so-called uncles taught her how to shoot every weapon known to man as well as how to hotwire a car and break into security systems, I don't know what he has to worry about. But this is how love works. It makes people do weird things.

"Can you shush about the tequila already? Some of us can't drink at all, but you don't hear us whining and complaining," Suzie says.

Hailey rolls her eyes. "Not right now, but there's been plenty of whining and complaining."

"Whatever." Suzie points to me. "You were going to tell us what happened to bring you to Milwaukee."

"It's not some big exciting secret like having a stalker or a gang after me."

I'm not pulling these examples out of thin air. Hailey had a stalker, and Faith had a gang after her.

"I got fired is all."

Faith gasps. "You got fired? But they love you. You're the hardest worker they have."

"Had. Fired, remember?"

Suzie rubs her hands together. "What did you do? Did you photocopy your chest and paste copies on the walls everywhere? Or did you write an erotic romance and accidentally send it to the entire client list?"

I laugh. "You've got quite the imagination. Maybe you should write an erotic romance."

"Grayson won't let me," she pouts. "He doesn't want me telling the entire world about our sex life. As if I don't have an imagination."

Faith grasps my hand and squeezes. "What happened?"

I sigh. "I might have accidentally overheard one of the lawyers call a client a bad name and I might have then accidentally called the lawyer out for his language in front of the entire firm during a meeting. And then this lawyer might have gotten a bit angry and called me a bad name in front of everyone. And then I might have yelled at him and told him where he could shove his job."

I'm not proud of it, but I lost my temper. I'm used to the lawyers I work for being arrogant snobs, but there's a limit to how much I will accept. And using racist and sexual slurs is my hard limit.

"Good for you," Phoebe says and everyone else murmurs their agreement. "Women shouldn't put up with men's crap anymore."

"I told you what happened. Can we move on to another topic now, please?" I plead.

Everyone agrees, and I actually manage to enjoy the rest of the night despite feeling Barney's eyes burning a hole in my back the entire time. What's his problem anyway?

Chapter 4

A couple are on a date at a fancy restaurant. The woman tells the man to say something to get her heart racing. He replies, "I forgot my wallet."

Barney

I force a smile on my face before strolling into McGraw's on Saturday afternoon. I love the pub and I love my brothers, but right now I don't want to be here. Not when I know my brothers haven't missed what's going on between Val and me.

"What does the receptionist at a sperm bank say as clients leave?" I ask as I join the group.

I waggle my eyebrows. "Thanks for coming!"

I raise my fist and Sid bumps it with his. "How's Mary Ann?"

Mary Ann is Sid's sixth wife if you can believe it. We're hoping this one is going to stick.

Sid grins. "She's good. Pulling a double shift today."

Mary Ann is an emergency room nurse. Sid met her when Phoebe's first husband decided to distract us by setting fire to his house to allow him a chance to kidnap Phoebe. While we were rushing Sid to the hospital, Ryker found Phoebe.

"When's Wally back from his honeymoon?" I ask Lenny.

"Tomorrow."

I rub my hands together. "Any ideas for a prank?"

Lenny smirks. "Chrissie and I have it all set up already."

"Chrissie? You're talking to Wally's wife while they're on their honeymoon?" Wally will not be amused when he finds out.

Lenny shrugs. "She called me."

"How's Faith?" I ask Max.

He chuckles. "You can throw questions at us all day, but it won't stop us from giving you shit about Valerie."

I shrug. "There's nothing to give me shit about. There is no Valerie and me."

"Brother, Valerie isn't her."

My body tightens at the thought of Valerie. The woman is everything I love in a woman. For starters, she's gorgeous. She has curves that go on for days – curves my hands itch to touch – and these bright blue eyes. They're usually filled with laughter and mischief. And her brown hair feels soft as silk in my fingers.

And then there's her personality. She's always smiling and up to no good. Like I said. Right up my alley.

But I'm not in the market for a woman. I don't deserve love and happiness after what I did.

Lenny claps his hand on my shoulder. "It's not your fault. You can't shoulder the blame for what happened to Ruby for the rest of your life. I repeat. It wasn't your fault."

At the mention of my wife, guilt crashes down on me. I growl and whirl around on Lenny. "Whose fault was it then?"

He holds up his hands. "No one's, brother. It was no one's fault."

He's wrong. It has to be someone's fault. Otherwise, why did it happen? Why did I lose my wife if not because I wasn't paying enough attention to her?

"Take it from someone who's been there, you can't live in the past forever," Sid says.

Sid lost his first wife, too. Except his wife is alive and well. He just doesn't know *where* she is, because the bitch took off while he was deployed in a warzone. Sid went AWOL to get back to her before she left him, but he was too late. By the time he made it home, she'd packed up her stuff and was gone. The single item remaining in the house was a set of divorce papers.

"I'm not living in the past. Avoiding making the same mistake is learning from my past, not living in it."

Max barks out a laugh. "You're full of shit. You're running scared."

I cross my arms over my chest and glare at him. "I am not scared."

I'm fucking terrified. The way my body tightens whenever Valerie is near is scary enough as it is, but I also have this inexplicable need to protect her and keep her safe. Which is why I need to stay far, far away from the woman. She could destroy me, and she doesn't even realize it.

"I've got Valentine's Day," Lenny says.

I glare at him. My brothers will bet on anything. Usually, I am the first on board the betting plan. Not this time.

"I won't have you betting about Valerie and me."

Sid winks. "Then, you admit there's a Valerie and you?"

"Stop trying to catch me out. There is no Valerie and me. I will never be serious about another woman again in my life."

After how I failed Ruby, I don't deserve to find love again. I've made my peace with it. Or, at least I thought I had until Valerie strolled into the pub on Thanksgiving and my mind short-circuited.

"Are we going to stand around and gossip like old fish wives or are we going to drink some beer and play pool?" I ask when I notice Lenny open his mouth to speak, probably to contradict me again.

Lenny shrugs. "I'm up for taking all your money in a game of poker."

Max pours me a beer and sets it on the bar in front of me. "Then, you aren't going to do anything about this situation in Saint Louis?"

My brow furrows. "What situation in Saint Louis? We dealt with those gangs to keep Faith safe. Did something else happen? Do we need to go down there and kick some gangbanger ass?"

"I'm in," Sid declares. "Things are getting boring around here."

Lenny slaps him upside the head. "What is wrong with you? We literally caught a traitor who was stalking Chrissie a week ago. Is Mary Ann not satisfying your needs? Do I need to help?" He licks his lips as he scans Sid's body.

Lenny's bisexual. He pretends to hit on one of us on a regular basis. He's not serious. He would never shit where he eats, but he loves to make us feel uncomfortable. I'm not uncomfortable. I could care less what Lenny gets up to in his bedroom. Although, when he takes three men home at one time, I admit the logistics of how it all works confuses me. I'll never ask him to explain, though. Too much information.

Sid pushes Lenny. "Knock it off. You're talking about my wife, not some floozy. It's none of your business what we get up to in our marital bed."

"Marital bed?" I snort. "How old are you again, Sid?"

"Fifty-seven. Same as you, you little bastard."

I puff out my chest. "Who are you calling little?"

We're both several inches over six-foot, but whereas I'm a lean, mean fighting machine, Sid is a broad bulldozer. He thinks being bigger gives him an advantage. He's wrong.

Sid dances on his toes like he's readying for a fight. "You think you can take me, huh?"

I kick out my leg to knock him off balance before wrapping an arm around his neck and putting him into a chokehold.

Max slams his hands down on the bar. "Knock it off, children. We have a serious situation to discuss."

I freeze. Max doesn't screw around. If he says a situation is serious, it's serious. I loosen my hold on Sid, and he shoves me away.

"What is it?"

Max rubs a hand down his face. "I don't know the details."

I step closer to the bar. "What do you know?"

"I know Valerie got fired after she confronted one of the attorneys at the law firm she was working at in Saint Louis."

"Confronted? Confronted how?"

I've barely known Valerie for a month, but I know the woman is fearless. She'd race headfirst into trouble without blinking an eye. What the hell has she got herself into?

"Is she hiding out in Milwaukee?" It's what Faith did when her kid Ollie got into trouble with a local gang.

Max shrugs. "I don't know the details."

"Does Faith know? Can you ask her?"

He smirks. "I tried." Judging from the sparkle in his eye, I can guess exactly what his efforts consisted of.

"I can go talk to her," Lenny offers. I have my hand wrapped around his neck before the word 'her' is out of his mouth.

"You aren't going to Valerie's home to talk to her." My words are barely understandable since my jaw is locked up tight.

Lenny raises his hands. "Okay," he chokes out.

I drop my hand and step back. "I'm on my way."

"Keep us informed," Sid orders.

I wave to acknowledge I heard him, but I don't slow down.

"Remember Barney, Val isn't Ruby," Max shouts before I can get out the door.

I don't bother acknowledging him. I've got bigger problems than comparing Ruby with Valerie right now. Val in danger? Not if I can help it. And, lucky for her, I can help.

Chapter 5

What did one boat say to the other boat? Are you interested in a little row-mance?

I sigh when the doorbell rings on Saturday afternoon. I saw every single person I know in the city besides my boss yesterday at the bar. Who could possibly be here now? And, more importantly, do I want to see whoever it is?

I spy Barney through the peephole. It's official. I do not want to see who it is at the door. The warmth in my stomach at the sight of Barney calls me a liar. I ignore it. What does my stomach know anyway?

Bang. Bang. "I know you're in there, Val. Open up."

Ugh. What does he want this time? I really don't need to have 'the talk' with him again. I get it. You're not interested. Stop knocking on my door then, will ya?

"Valerie's not available right now. If you leave your name and number, she'll get back to you as soon as possible. Beep."

"Very funny, Trouble. Now open this door. Or I'll open it for you."

Who does he think he is? The Big Bad Wolf in the "Three Little Pigs" story? The building is made of brick. Even the Big Bad Wolf can't blow down a brick building.

"This is your last warning."

Oooh, my last warning. I'm sooo scared. I cross my arms over my chest to await his response. I hear another door in the hallway open.

"What are you doing?" An old lady asks.

Shoot. Faith warned me about the nosy old lady when I moved into her apartment. And while I'm fine with nosy old biddies – what is she going to do? Hit me with her cane? – Faith is technically the tenant of this apartment for a few more days. I don't want her getting a call about some man disturbing the peace in her apartment.

I open the door and yank Barney inside. "How did you find out my address?" I ask before he can speak.

"I helped Max move Faith and Ollie out when she moved in with him."

Of course, he did. I should have known.

He frowns as he studies my apartment. "I can't believe Faith lived here with Ollie. This place is a dump."

I plant my hands on my hips. "But it's good enough for me?"

To be honest, the place is kind of a dump. The walls are paper thin, the heating doesn't work half the time, and the warm water doesn't last long enough to fill the bathtub. It has one thing going for it, though. It's cheap. Staying here for the next year will give me a chance to save up some money. I've always wanted to buy a home, but I've never been able to put aside enough money for a down payment. Living here is the perfect opportunity to make my dream happen.

Barney clears his throat. "I didn't mean it like it sounded."

"Whatever," I huff. "What are you doing here?"

"We need to talk."

I throw my head back and scream. Not for long. I don't want Ms. Nosy Old Lady calling the police on me.

"Are you kidding me with this? I get it. You don't want a relationship. Enough already. I promise not to chase you anymore." I stomp to the door and throw it open. "Now, get out."

Barney marches over and for a second I think he's going to leave and let this go. I should be so lucky. He slams the door before squeezing my shoulder. "I'm not here to discuss us."

"Because there is no us," I remind him. The tingling his hand on my body is causing calls me a liar. This man doesn't want us, I remind my body. Judging by all my nerve endings flaring to life, my body is snubbing my reminder.

I step forward until his hand falls. And I don't miss the feeling of his hand on my body at all. Not me. "What do you want?"

"What happened in Saint Louis?"

I freeze at his question. What does he know? How does he know? Actually, the how is easy. Faith. Doesn't she know she can't trust Max to not tell his brothers her secrets? The group of five former military men is worse than a bunch of old ladies with all their gossiping.

I cross my arms over my chest, and I notice Barney's gaze dip to my breasts. I'm what romance novels call voluptuous. I'd rather be skinny like Faith, but no amount of dieting has helped reduce the size of my chest one teensy bit. I've learned to live with it. Besides, having a chest men can't keep their eyes off does have its advantages.

"What are you talking about?" I ask and Barney rips his gaze away from my chest.

"You got fired."

At his statement, my arms drop and my shoulders slump. It's bad enough I got fired, but now everyone is going to know. I didn't do anything wrong but fired is fired. No one wants to say they've been fired no matter how it came about. I feel like a failure.

"It's none of your business."

Barney's nostrils flare. "If you're in danger, it damn well is my business."

What in the world is he talking about? I'm not in danger. In danger of being embarrassed to death? Yes. In danger as in someone coming after me? I think not.

"I'm not in danger."

"You can't be certain you aren't in danger. You confronted an attorney. A defense attorney whose job it is to get criminals off for crimes they committed."

"Hey now! You're being awful judgy. Defense attorneys are an essential part of the judicial system."

He snorts. "If they work for the poor and underrepresented, but you worked for one of those fancy law firms that ensure the wealthy and affluent get a slap on the wrist for committing horrendous crimes such as rape and manslaughter."

Huh. He's a crusader. Who knew?

"We can debate the merit of defense attorneys all day and night."

Trust me. I've heard it all. I've worked for defense attorneys for more than twenty years. There's nothing he can throw at me I haven't heard before.

"It doesn't matter. I'm not in danger." I blow out a puff of air and tell him what happened. "My boss called his client a racist, sexist name and I called him on it. The story ends there. No danger involved whatsoever."

"A racist, sexist name?"

I roll my eyes. "Do you need me to spell it out for you?" Because spelling is all I will do. I don't say either of the words out loud. Unless I'm screaming my head off at my boss, apparently.

Barney nods.

"The N-word and the C-word."

"I agree it's not okay for a man to use those words when referring to a woman, but you can't be calling your boss out for using them."

"Why not? Someone has to." Remaining silent is being complicit. And I refuse to be complicit.

"Because it's dangerous."

"Dude, I do what I want to do, when I want to. No one tells me what to do."

"I will damn well tell you what to do if your actions

are dangerous."

"You don't own me because your tongue has been in my mouth," I snarl.

He prowls toward me and I back up until I hit the wall next to the door. Heat flares in his eyes and my body comes alive. My breasts feel heavy, and my nipples tingle. This man and how my body responds to him is dangerous. I'm not afraid of a little danger, though.

His hands slap against the wall next to my head and my legs weaken. Holy Toledo is the man sex on a stick, and I want to take a bite out of him. Which is exactly what I do. I lean forward and nip his bottom lip.

Barney growls before his hand tangles in my hair, his head descends, and his lips slam onto mine. This is not a gentle kiss. Both of us are too worked up for gentle. And who needs gentle anyway? Not this girl.

"Open up for me," he demands, and I don't hesitate to obey.

As soon as his taste of the outdoors, beer, and a flavor unique to Barney hits me, I go wild. I squeeze his shoulders letting my nails dig in. Despite the layers of cloths separating us, I know he feels the sharp sting when he groans down my throat.

My hands travel down his back to reach his ass. Barney is tall and lean, but he's not some skinny man. His muscles are hard and defined. I knead his ass and he thrusts into my tummy.

At the feel of his hardness, I hitch a leg over his hip and grind myself into him. I moan and feel myself getting wet.

Barney tears his mouth away from mine and I let my head fall back. It hits the wall with a thump, but I couldn't care less about hitting my head right now. Not when Barney's lips are trailing down my neck. He reaches the junction between my neck and shoulder and bites down.

"Yes," I hiss.

He freezes before I hear him swear. He lifts his head and I open my eyes to find panic in his eyes. Why is he afraid of me? I'm a woman, not a freaking terrorist.

He untangles himself from me and retreats forcing me to drop my leg and my hands. I wobble and he places a hand on my hip to steady me.

"I'm sorry, Val." His hand drops and without his body covering mine, it suddenly feels cold in my apartment.

"It's fine, Barney. Leave and run away. You're good at it, after all."

A muscle in his jaw ticks, but he reaches for the door and opens it. He looks back. "I am sorry."

I wave away his concern. "Whatever."

I wait until he's left to lock the door and switch off the lights. *Enough, Val. Enough.* No more chasing Barney, and there will certainly be no more kissing the man no matter how good his kisses feel.

Chapter 6

Love is getting mad at someone, telling that person to go to hell, and hoping they get there safely.

I stomp over to the bar where Faith and Max are hanging out at McGraw's Pub. Faith catches sight of me and her eyes widen before she hides behind Max who appears amused with the situation. I, however, am not amused.

I cross my arms over my chest. "How dare you tell everyone about what happened in Saint Louis?"

Faith peeks her head out from behind her husband. "To be fair, I don't know all the details of what happened, so I couldn't have told anyone about them."

"Semantics," I growl. "Do you think I want the whole world knowing I got fired?"

Faith steps away from Max. "Are you serious? You got fired for standing up for someone. You shouldn't be ashamed of it."

I'm not ashamed. I'd do it again in a second. But everyone knowing I got fired is embarrassing. And, okay, fine. Maybe I'm a little bit ashamed.

"You stood up for someone?" Ollie asks.

"The lawyer called his client a bad name," I kind of explain. I'm not saying those two nasty words again.

"Then, it's good you stood up for her." Ollie nods. "But it's wrong you got fired. You should sue them."

I cock an eyebrow. "Sue lawyers? I'm not rich, Ollie boy." I ruffle his hair and he slaps at my hands.

"I'm not a kid anymore. I'm sixteen."

Faith sighs. "And don't I know it." She throws an

arm around me. "Are we good now?" She bats her eyelashes at me.

I shove her away. "Your feminine wiles don't work on me. Try them on your husband."

"Oh no! Please don't," Phoebe begs as she arrives.

"Hey, Pops," Hailey says as she enters. "Do you need me to cover you so you can have a break with your fiancée?" She waggles her eyebrows.

Ollie feigns gagging. "You suck as a step-sister. You're supposed to be on my side. Not theirs."

Hailey taps her chin. "No, I don't think so. I'm supposed to tease you and embarrass you." She wraps an arm around his neck and gives him a noogie.

Ollie fights her off. "I'm going back upstairs to my room."

"Don't forget to let Pepper out," Max yells at his retreating figure.

Pepper is Ollie's brown lab. Max bought the puppy to secure Ollie's love. I wish one of my step-fathers would have tried to buy my love. I would have settled for 'nice' to be honest.

"I am not ready for teenagers," Phoebe says as she stares at Ollie's retreating form.

Ryker kisses her forehead. "You have thirteen years to prepare."

Phoebe's face pales, and she gulps. "I didn't think this whole having children thing through."

Faith pats her hand. "If anyone thought it through, the human race would die off."

"I thought it through and I'm having six kids," Suzie announces as she joins the group.

"What are you trying to do? Start your own football team?" Hailey asks.

Suzie hip checks Hailey and ends up bouncing off her and wheeling backwards. Grayson catches her before she can fall on her ass on the floor. "You need to be more careful, Munchkin."

"I am careful. I can't help it Hailey's hips are made of stone."

Hailey pats her hips. "You wish—"

Aiden slaps a hand over her mouth before she can finish. "No taunting the pregnant lady."

Suzie throws a hand in the air. "Yes! It's in the rule book now. No taunting Suzie while she's pregnant."

"But Suzie's planning to be pregnant for the rest of her life," Hailey whines.

"You could always get pregnant," Aiden suggests.

Hailey glares up at him. "Have you not listened? Phoebe is throwing up all day and night at the office. No thanks."

Aiden's mouth settles into a straight line.

I wiggle my eyebrows. "I'd have Aiden's babies." I lick my lips as I look the man up and down. Dark hair, strong jaw, blue eyes, and beard all wrapped up in a six-foot-three muscled package. Aiden is one hot man.

Actually, all of my friends' husbands are sexy as all get out. Ryker may appear a bit scary at six-foot-six with a big bushy beard, but his green eyes are kind. Although Grayson is shorter than the others at five-foot-ten, he's still hot as Hades with his whisky-colored eyes, broad shoulders, and dimpled cheeks.

Unfortunately, they're all way too young for me. Oh, and they're all in committed relationships. With my friends. Doesn't mean I can't look, though. I do love me some eye candy.

The door bangs open, and Chrissie and Wally stroll in. Suzie squeals and rushes to them. "Tell us all about it. Did he drive you to bone town for your honeymoon?" She waggles his eyebrows. "Did you leave your room at all during the entire time?"

Wally kisses Chrissie's forehead and she nearly melts into him. My gaze drifts away from them and finds

Barney who's already staring at me. I notice the heat in his eyes and glance away. The man has run from me twice now after kissing me silly. I'd be an absolute idiot to read anything into his look.

Wally saunters over to the uncles' table where Barney, Lenny, and Sid are seated. They clap him on the back and give him their congratulations before Max arrives with a round of beers for the group.

Suzie grabs Chrissie's hand and drags her toward a table on the other side of the room. "Scram," she tells her husband. "It's time for girl talk."

You don't have to tell him twice. Grayson, Ryker, and Aiden practically sprint to the pool tables in the back room when they hear the words 'girl talk'.

Suzie winks at me. "Gets them every time."

We settle at the table. Chrissie is literally glowing. She keeps glancing over her shoulder to look at Wally who can't keep his eyes off of her. I predict it'll be an early night for the two of them.

"And," Suzie prompts. "Tell us everything. Wally looks like the type of man who will study every erogenous zone in your body and figure out how to give you more pleasure than you've ever known before."

Chrissie's cheeks darken. "Wally is a good study."

Suzie claps. "Oh goodie. Details!"

"No! No details. Wally is like a dad to me." Phoebe covers her eyes. As if covering your eyes helps to stop her from hearing.

"Don't worry. Dads have sex, too." Chrissie winks.

Phoebe's hands drop and she gags. "I think I'm going to be sick."

I roll my eyes at her. "You're not exactly pure as the driven snow. You're pregnant, which proves you are more than aware of how slot A fits into B."

Suzie's hand shoots into the air, and we high-five.

"Where did you go anyway?" Hailey asks.

"We went to …" Chrissie's voice tapers off as her eyes zero in on the entry to the pub. I glance behind me and notice her friend Lexi. "Excuse me," Chrissie says and stands.

She's delusional if she thinks this group isn't going to follow her and be all up in her business. I've barely known them longer than a month and I know better.

"What are you doing here?" Chrissie asks Lexi.

Lexi rears back. "What do you mean? Am I not welcome here?" Her gaze drifts over to the uncles' table where Lenny is staring at her like she's a big juicy steak and he's been on a strict vegetarian diet for years. I'm surprised he's not licking his lips. Things are getting interesting.

Chrissie hauls Lexi in for a hug. "Of course, you're welcome," she says when she releases her. "I assumed you'd be back at work by now is all."

"Your husband asked me to watch over your house and cat while you were away."

Chrissie raises an eyebrow at Wally who shrugs in response. "He didn't tell me."

I have a feeling there's a lot Wally doesn't tell his wife. I, for one, wouldn't put up with it. I can't handle secrets. Secrets lead to lies and lies lead to betrayal.

Wally stands and saunters over to us. He kisses Chrissie's hair. "I'm sorry I didn't tell you. I guess I had other things on my mind."

Suzie rubs her hands together. "Now, we're getting somewhere."

Wally ruffles her hair. "Hey, kid. How's the baby growing going?"

Suzie's hand caresses her baby bump and she smiles up at him. "Perfect. Everything's perfect."

"Happy for you, kid," he says before starting toward the hallway leading to the restrooms.

When Suzie opens her mouth to speak, Chrissie places a finger over her lips to quiet her. She motions toward Barney, Sid, and Lenny who stand with boxes in their hands. They travel the room handing out whatever's in the box to the patrons.

My brow wrinkles when I notice everyone putting on multi-colored clown wigs and red noses. Hailey leans close to whisper, "Wally's terrified of clowns."

Big, bad Wally? The super-secret spy? Is afraid of clowns? This is going to be good.

We stand on the side of the room where we have a view of the hallway. Wally strolls out of the restroom a few minutes later. His face lights up when he notices Chrissie waiting for him. I hold my breath as I watch the two of them walk into the bar.

The music changes to *Tears of a Clown* and everyone in the room turns in Wally's direction. He comes to a screeching halt before shouting, "What the hell?"

Chrissie is bent over laughing her ass off. Wally picks her up and throws her over his shoulder. He flicks his wrist at the room as he opens the door and marches outside. The door slams shut, but everyone can hear as Chrissie shouts at him, "This is what you get for surprising me with a wedding and honeymoon."

Guess I'm not the only one who doesn't appreciate secrets.

Chapter 7

A husband and wife are drinking wine at home. The wife says, "I love you." The husband asks if it's her or the wine talking. She replies, "It's me talking to the wine."

I rush into McGraw's Pub at 10 p.m. It's New Year's Eve and the party is going strong. I had planned on arriving hours earlier, but my boss – aka Mr. Davenport the Dick – kept throwing work at me until I put my foot down and told him I'd see him on the second of January. He glared at me for a long moment before finally agreeing I could leave.

"You made it!" Faith shouts and throws her arms around me.

I have to lock my legs to stop us from crashing to the floor. Someone's had a few drinks this evening. Time for me to catch up.

"Sorry, I'm late. Mr. Dickhead is preparing for a big trial starting next week and the asswipe apparently doesn't have a life," I explain as I steady Faith and ensure she can stand on her own two feet before letting her go.

I hear a growl behind me and whirl around to find Barney glaring at me. "What's your problem, Mr. Grumpy?"

"Don't go antagonizing your boss."

I roll my eyes and turn away from him. I follow orders from no man, let alone a man who runs hot and cold. Talk about brain freeze. I shrug off my coat and hang it on my arm. I hear a grunt before the coat is whipped away from my arm and thrown over my shoulders. What the hell? I yank the coat off of me.

Barney tries to grab the coat from me. "Keep it on," he grumbles.

I manage to wrench the coat from his fingers. "I'm not cold, Mom. But thanks."

"You're half naked."

"I'm dressed for a New Year's Eve party because guess what? It's New Year's Eve."

I'm wearing a silver top. From the front, it's a perfectly respectable sleeveless shiny silver top. From the back, though, it's downright naughty as there is no back except for a strap around my neck and at my waist. The contraption I have to wear to keep my boobs from sagging to my knees is more complicated to get on than a high school calculus exam, but the way Barney's eyes flare with heat makes the discomfort worth it.

I whirl around to give Barney my back. When he growls, my body tingles in all the right places. I memorize the sound before lacing my arm through Faith's. "Lead the way, bar wench."

She guides me to a high-top table on the side of the bar where all our friends are. Hailey hands me a shot glass. "This better not be tequila."

She shakes her head, but I sniff the liquid just in case. It smells lemony. I throw it back. "It's yummy."

She waggles her eyebrows at me. "You're looking mighty sexy tonight."

Faith bumps my shoulder. "Barney thought so, too."

"I am totally winning this bet."

Chrissie wags her finger at her. "There are barely two hours remaining in the day. I'm totally winning this bet."

Lexi's gaze ping-pongs back and forth between them. "What bet? What's going on?"

I roll my eyes. "They bet on when Barney and I will 'get together'." As if the event will ever happen.

Phoebe frowns. "I totally lost. I thought they'd hop into bed together before Thanksgiving dinner was over."

Lexi's eyes widen. "Your Thanksgiving dinners

sound a lot different than mine."

Chrissie snorts. "Are you serious? You practically force fed me moonshine when I was at your house for the holidays."

Lexi shrugs. "I can't help it you're a lightweight when it comes to moonshine."

Hailey leans forward. "Chrissie a lightweight? You're kidding, right? The woman drank me under the table."

Lexi barks out a laugh. "Don't come to West Virginia then. You wouldn't stand a chance."

"Aiden!" Hailey shouts across the room. "We're going to West Virginia on our next vacation."

"Will you wear a bikini?" Aiden asks across the room as if not everyone is listening to them. She nods. "Then, we're going to West Virginia."

Hailey throws her arms in the air. "Yeah!" She leans close to whisper. "I don't own a bikini."

The door to the pub bangs open, and Lenny stomps in. He's covered from head to toe in confetti. "You!" He points to Wally. "I will get you back."

"Who wants to know how Lenny ended up covered in confetti?" Suzie asks.

My hand flies into the air. "And how."

Chrissie leans forward. "It's easy really. You fill the front vents in a car with confetti. When the defrost or heat is switched on – boom! Confetti everywhere."

"Where have you been all my life?" I'm serious. I need to know all her tricks.

"You don't want to know," she scowls.

"I've got Valentine's Day," Phoebe shouts, and I rear back at the volume of her voice.

"I've already got Valentine's Day," Hailey says.

Faith's brow wrinkles. "I thought you had New Year's Eve."

Hailey waves a hand in dismissal. "No, not for Val

and Barney." She points to Lenny who can't keep his eyes off Lexi. "For him."

"I'm confused," Phoebe says. "Isn't Lenny bi-sexual?"

"Bi-sexual," Hailey repeats. "It means he's into men and women alike. And right now, he's got his sights set on Lexi girl."

Lexi holds up her hands. "Um, I don't live here, remember?"

Chrissie snorts. "Like I don't know you already quit your job."

This is news to me. I watch the two friends as they seem to have some type of silent conversation.

"I told you telepathy exists," Suzie shouts.

Max arrives and sets a tray of orange-colored shots with sugary rims on the table. "I didn't expect the pub to serve glimmery shots," I say as I grab one of the glasses.

Max smiles down at Faith. "Someone convinced me the ladies like shiny things."

"He's giving her goo-goo eyes. Someone stop them before they kiss," Phoebe squeals.

Ryker arrives and palms her neck before sipping at her lips. Phoebe sighs and he deepens the kiss.

"For someone who complains an awful lot about other people making out in front of her, she doesn't seem to have a problem with public affection," I say in a loud voice so Phoebe can hear me.

Phoebe drags herself away from her husband. "It's his fault. My mind goes mushy when he's near."

"I know what you mean," Faith says with her eyes focused on Max.

As much as I'm happy for Faith for finding her love and am all for couples and such, it's New Year's Eve. I don't want to stand around and watch couples make goo-goo eyes at each other. I want to party.

I scan the bar and realize the stage used for Chrissie and Wally's wedding is back and a band is set up on it. As I look on, three men and one woman saunter out and pick up their instruments.

"Are you ready to party?" the woman shouts into the microphone before the drums and guitars start up.

I grab Faith's hand and drag her to the makeshift dancefloor. Hailey, Chrissie, and Lexi follow us while Ryker and Grayson hold back their women. I giggle as Suzie pushes Grayson off before grasping Phoebe's hand and joining us.

"As if I can't dance because I'm pregnant," Suzie huffs.

Hailey laughs. "You couldn't dance before you were pregnant."

Suzie sticks her tongue out at her before she begins dancing and proves Hailey's point. Is the woman having a seizure? As long as she's having fun, I say 'have at it'.

I throw my hands in the air and shake my booty. I close my eyes and feel the music. I love to dance. But there are never enough opportunities to dance anymore. I'm forty-five years old. I can't exactly spend my weekends in nightclubs anymore. Plus, who would go with me? I may be an independent woman, but I draw the line at going out on my own.

By the time five minutes to midnight rolls around, I'm hot and sweaty and feeling all kinds of happy. I've got my girls all around me. Wait. Where are my girls? I search the room and discover the men have claimed their women as the clock counts down to midnight.

But where's Lexi? She's not involved with anyone. I do another scan of the room and notice Lenny has her cornered in the back room. Interesting. Maybe I should get in on the bet about the two of them.

I feel a hand on my lower back and goosebumps break out on my skin. The hand exerts pressure until I turn around to face Barney.

"I'm not kissing you at midnight," I shout at him.

He frowns. "Do you have a ride home?"

I jiggle my phone at him. "I'll call a ride when I'm ready to go."

He leans close to whisper in my ear. "It'll be hours before you can get a ride. Let me take you home." I cock an eyebrow. "As an apology."

Before I can respond, the noise level in the bar rises as the countdown nears its end. "Ten. Nine. Eight. Seven. Six. Five. Four. Three. Two. One. Happy New Year!"

Silver and white balloons fall from the ceiling. When my gaze meets Barney's, his eyes flare before he wraps an arm around my waist and drags me near. His lips descend and meet mine. Despite knowing I should fight him, I don't. I open my lips and allow him to plunder my mouth.

He growls and rips his lips from mine. "I'm taking you home."

I don't know if his words are a threat or a promise, but I can't wait to find out either way.

Chapter 8

Is your name Wi-Fi? Because I'm really feeling a connection.

Barney

Despite the adrenaline coursing through my veins, I force myself to drive the speed limit and obey the traffic signs. I'm probably one of the few people on the road at this time who hasn't been drinking. The second Valerie entered McGraw's with her back on display I switched to water. No way was I letting another man bring her home.

And there were plenty of contenders. Half the bar couldn't keep their eyes off her as she shimmied on the dance floor. Everyone held their breath hoping and praying her top would shift to reveal her glorious breasts. Breasts I can't wait to see with my own two eyes.

Lucky for the men in the bar, her shirt never allowed a glimpse of her chest. I'd have been forced to kill each and every one of them if it had.

We reach Val's apartment building and I frown as I park the car. I wish she didn't live here. The security door doesn't work half the time and the locks on her apartment door are a joke. The neighborhood isn't half bad, but it's not the best. I know she makes decent money as a legal secretary. Why then is she living here? Is she hiding a secret?

I've had enough of secrets in the past years. Between Phoebe hiding her true identity, Faith keeping her situation in Saint Louis a secret, and Chrissie not coming clean about her past, there has been entirely too much danger surrounding the people I consider family. I didn't sacrifice more than two decades of my life in the military for my loved ones to be at risk.

Valerie reaches for the door handle, but I place a hand on her wrist to stop her. "Wait there."

She rolls her eyes. "Wait here? I'm not some nineteenth-century damsel. I can open my own car door."

My hand tightens on her wrist. "I'm not saying you can't open your car door. I'm trying to be a gentleman."

Her nose scrunches in confusion, and my jaw tightens. Has no one ever treated her like a lady before? I hop out of my truck and rush around the front to open her door for her.

I bow. "Milady."

She giggles and warmth rushes through me. I love the sound of her happiness. I grasp her hand and lead her into the building and up the stairs to her apartment. When we reach the door, she whirls around.

"Thank you for giving me a ride home."

Does she think she's going to get rid of me this easily? I motion to her door. "Open it. I need to check if your apartment is safe."

She rolls her eyes before unlocking the door and motioning me in. I know it's overkill, but after everything I've gone through in the past years with my friends, I can't stop myself from checking all of the rooms are clear.

When I return to the living room, Val is in the kitchen drinking a glass of water. She lifts her glass in silent question, but I shake my head. I've been drinking water for two hours now. I don't need any more.

She places the glass on the counter and walks to the door. "Thanks again."

Before she can open the door, I stop her. "I need to apologize."

She waves a hand. "It's all good."

When she tries to open the door again, I squeeze her shoulder and spin her around. She gasps as she gazes up at me. The sparkle of interest in her eyes is an invitation I can't refuse. I slam my lips down on hers. She tastes of cherry lip gloss and lemon from the glitter vodka shots she drank all evening. I moan as the delicious combination hits me.

I plunder her mouth in an attempt to explore every single inch while my hands thread through her hair. I love her hair. It's long enough to fist, but not too long that it gets in the way and it feels soft as silk. I tighten my hands and use my grip to tilt her head to allow me to dive deeper into her mouth.

I prowl forward until her legs hit the sofa. Her fingers clench on my ass as she nearly falls onto her back. On her back is exactly where I want her. I release my hold on her hair and wrench my mouth from her lips before picking her up and laying her down on the sofa.

I stand and stare down at the beauty laid out before me. Her chest heaves up and down as she tries to catch her breath and I decide I can't wait one more second before I see her naked breasts.

"Arms up," I order. I grasp the hem of her shirt and drag it off of her.

The cups of her black bra barely contain her breasts. I glide a finger along the hem and watch as goosebumps appear in my wake.

"This needs to come off," I tell her.

She smirks before sitting up. "Have at it."

I reach around, but instead of finding one strap with a clasp to undo, there are several crisscrossing each other. "What the hell? Is this some medieval torture device?"

"Ha! You aren't the one who had to wear it all night."

"The way you looked tonight … it was worth it."

She helps me unhook the fastenings before laying down once again. My hands dig under the shoulder straps and I draw them down her arms until the bra cups fall forward to reveal her breasts.

"You're magnificent."

I grasp the fabric between her breasts and pull it away to view her chest in all its glory. And I do mean glory. Her breasts are large, more than a handful, and I've always been partial to big-breasted women. The more for me to play with. And it's time to play.

I study her face as I knead her breasts. Her eyes close and her head falls back as she arches into my hands. I don't wait to give her what she's silently begging for. I lick the soft skin around the areola; making sure to avoid her nipple. She squirms and rubs her legs together.

"Stop torturing me," she hisses.

I pause what I'm doing to glance up at her. Her bright, blue eyes are nearly black with need. "But you're enjoying it."

She glares at me and I cock an eyebrow before bending down to nip at her nipple. She moans and her hands fly to my head to keep me right where I am. I lick and suck and nip at her breasts until her squirming nearly throws me off the sofa.

Only then do I move on by trailing kisses down her belly until I reach the waistband of her pants. I snap open the button and lower the zipper. She lifts her butt to help me lower her pants and underwear down her legs. I take my time; knowing I'm driving her crazy.

"Left leg over the back of the sofa," I order, and she doesn't hesitate to follow directions. Good. She usually fights me on every-damn-thing – something I normally get off on – but I'm in charge in the bedroom.

She's completely naked and open to me now. I slide my hands up her legs stopping at the juncture of her thighs before sliding them down again. She squirms and tries to close her legs, but I clamp my hands down on her thighs.

"No. Stay open for me."

"Then, stop teasing me," she grumbles.

I smirk. "How about this?" I dip my head until my

nose is near her opening. I sniff. She smells of vanilla and strawberries. Two of my favorite things.

Her fingers dig into my skull, and I decide I've teased her enough. My tongue sneaks out and I lick a circle around her clit. She moans and I get to work. I suck and lick around her clit until her legs are clamped around my head and she's riding my face.

"Are you going to come for me?" I ask before plunging two fingers into her opening. I curl them just right and she explodes.

"Yes!" Val shouts.

I continue to thrust my fingers in and out of her until her orgasm wanes and her legs drop open. After a few moments, her eyes open and she gazes down at me. Her smile is glorious.

"Now, it's my turn."

She smirks before knifing up and grabbing my collar to pull me into a kiss. She doesn't seem to mind the taste of herself on my lips. In fact, she moans and deepens the kiss before pressing on my shoulders until I fall back on the sofa.

She rips open my jeans and tugs them down my legs. My cock pops out and her hand fists me. She glides her hand up and down my length. When her wrist twists at the top, I groan. "Yes."

Her hand disappears and my eyes pop open to find Val straddling me. "Condom," I insist as she holds herself over me. "Wallet."

She grunts before finding my wallet in my jeans' pocket and removing a condom. She doesn't hesitate to rip open the package with her teeth and roll the protection down my length. She straddles me again and cocks an eyebrow as she holds herself over me. I nod and she slams herself down on me.

"Holy hell!" I yell as her warmth surrounds me.

I'm not exactly celibate, but I'm not a manwhore like Lenny either. It's been entirely too long since I sank my cock into a willing woman.

Valerie places her hands on my chest and uses the leverage to raise and lower herself on me. I grasp her hips to slow her down, but she isn't to be slowed. I watch as her breasts jiggle as she moves and can't resist the urge to cover one with my mouth.

As soon as my teeth touch her nipple, she tightens around me, and her movements become erratic. I feel the telltale tingling in my spine and clench my teeth to stop from coming.

"Get there," I order. "Get there now."

"I'm there. I'm there," she chants as she tightens even more around me.

My vision blurs as I explode with her. "Valerie!" I shout.

She collapses on top of me, and I realize I'm still wearing my shirt. I chuckle. "Happy New Year, Ruby."

Valerie freezes on top of me before jumping to her feet. She points to the door. "Get the eff out. I don't want to ever see your face again."

I stand and nearly trip over my pants around my ankles. "What's wrong?"

Her nostrils flare. "What's wrong? Who's Ruby?"

Ruby? How does she know about Ruby? I didn't tell her. How? Oh shit. I must have said her name. "I'm sorry. I didn't …"

I button up my pants and grab my coat. There's really nothing to say when you call the woman you just had sex with your dead wife's name.

I open the door but turn around to face her once more before I leave. "I really am sorry."

"And I really don't give a crap."

A Valentine for Valerie

Chapter 9

Why do painters always fall for their models? Because they love them with all of their art.

I straighten my spine before marching my butt to the door of McGraw's Pub the next day. It's New Year's Day and I've been invited to join my new friends for lunch at the pub. While I'm most definitely not excited to be in the presence of Barney, I'm not a chicken. I do not run from things. And I never ever run from a man. Even if he is a slimeball who called me another woman's name during sex.

The second I open the door, I realize I made the right choice because inside it's total and utter chaos. Yes. This is exactly what I need.

A brown dog bounds up to me and jumps up to say hello. I scratch behind his ears. "Hello, beautiful. What's your name?"

"*Her* name is Lola and she's dangerous," Phoebe whispers.

I kneel down to stare into the brown eyes of the happy dog. "You're not dangerous, are you?"

"She is. Trust me."

Lola freezes at the sound of Phoebe's voice. She whips her head around and sprints full tilt at Phoebe who's holding out her hands and screaming, "No, Lola! No!"

Before Lola can jump on Phoebe, Ryker appears out of nowhere and grunts, "Heel."

The dog falls to her belly. She whines and stares up at Phoebe with those big, brown puppy dog eyes.

"This dog really loves you."

Suzie laughs from behind Phoebe. "She loves her loves her. You catch my drift?" In case I missed her meaning, she starts thrusting her hips.

"Hailey," Ryker bellows.

Hailey comes running from the hallway. Her hair is a mess and her cheeks are flushed. If those things don't give her away, the zipping up of her jeans totally would. Someone's bringing in the New Year right. Go, Hailey!

"What is it, big guy?"

He points to the dog. "Lola attacked Phoebe again. I told you when Phoebe got pregnant, I will not stand for your dog attacking my pregnant wife."

Aiden growls as he comes up behind Hailey. "And I won't stand for you talking to my wife in that tone of voice."

Ryker and Aiden square up against each other. Ryker is three inches taller than Aiden, but Aiden's no slouch either at six-foot-three.

Suzie claps and shouts, "Fight! Fight! Fight!"

Grayson arrives and picks her up. She slaps at his shoulders as he carries her away. "But I want to see the fight," she argues.

He leans close and whispers into her ear. She stops fighting and melts into him. I smile as I observe them. I'm happy Suzie found a man who can handle her crazy. It's not easy. Trust me, I know.

Hailey forces her way between the two men. She slaps a hand on Aiden's chest and another on Ryker's. "Knock it off. It's New Year's Day. There will be no fighting today."

Ryker crosses his arms across his chest and glares down at her. "I'm serious, Hailey. Lola could knock Phoebe over in her enthusiasm. I won't allow Phoebe to be hurt. Especially not when she's pregnant."

Aiden growls, but Hailey slaps her hand against his chest. "You are entirely correct, big guy. I should have been paying attention to Lola. I got distracted." Aiden smirks. "It won't happen again."

"Yes, it will."

Hailey rolls her eyes. "I meant me not paying attention to Lola, not the other distraction stuff."

The door crashes open and Chrissie and Wally enter. "What's going on?" she asks when she notices the stand-off between Hailey, Aiden, and Ryker.

"Hailey's dog, Lola, tried to hump Phoebe, and Ryker promptly lost his mind and yelled at Hailey. Aiden didn't approve of his tone of voice and nearly got into a fight with him. Oh, and Hailey and Aiden got busy somewhere in the back."

Chrissie grins up at Wally. "No more climbing into the shower with me. We missed all the fun."

He winks at her. "You had fun in the shower."

She rolls her eyes at him but the smile on her face says he's not wrong.

"Leave it alone," Lexi says as she enters with Lenny hot on her heels.

"But you don't understand."

"Understand what?" I ask.

Lenny frowns at me. "Never mind." He glances once more at Lexi before sauntering off.

"What's going on? Are you okay?" Chrissie asks her friend.

Lexi waves her hand. "I'm fine. I can handle some old geezer."

I waggle my eyebrows. "Old geezer? I wouldn't mind handling the old geezer."

Lenny may be in his late fifties, but I wouldn't call him an old geezer. Not when he fills out his jeans in such a delectable way.

"I thought you had your own old geezer," Lexi says.

"I'm sorry to report you've been misinformed," I quip despite feeling my cheeks warm as I think about all the things a certain old geezer did to my body last night. Barney definitely knows how to make a woman happy. Except for the whole calling a woman by the wrong name thing. I mentally slap myself. *No more thinking about Barney, Val.*

Sid and his wife Mary Ann arrive next. Mary Ann smiles and waves to everyone. "What did we miss thus far?"

"Lenny is chasing Lexi. Aiden and Hailey had sex in the bathroom. In fact," I scan the room, "I think Suzie and Grayson are having sexy times back there right now."

Mary Ann sighs. "I love this place."

Sid grunts. "Don't be getting any ideas about bathroom sex. My back isn't what it used to be."

She bites her bottom lip and bats her eyelashes at him. "Your back seemed fine this morning."

Barney laughs from behind me. Damn it. When did he arrive? My tummy warms and my nerves tingle. My body seems to have forgotten he called us another woman's name last night.

"What's wrong, old man? Having trouble keeping up with your wife?" Barney teases.

"At least I have a woman to keep up with," Sid snarls at him.

Barney glances at me, and I suddenly find the floor the most interesting thing in the world. Broadcast to the world what happened last night, why don't you? I'm not ashamed. Really, I'm not. I'd prefer not to explain to everyone why Barney and I as a couple will never happen, though. And these nosy people will definitely want to know why we're not cozying up to each other today after last night.

Someone shrieks before Suzie launches herself at me. "You did it!"

She hugs me with all her might. Geez. For a tiny thing, she sure is strong. Once I manage to extract myself, I ask her, "What are you talking about?" And why isn't she in the back getting busy with Grayson?

"You and Barney had sex last night!" she screams, and Faith comes running out of the kitchen with Max hot on her heels.

Everyone gathers around me and Barney. I glare at him.

"You had to glance at me, didn't you? Typical man. Always bragging about his conquests."

"Hey! I didn't say a word."

"I finally won a bet!" Hailey shouts as she throws her hands in the air.

Chrissie crosses her arms over her chest and stares at Hailey until she yelps, and her hands drop. "What? Why are you giving me the look?"

"You had New Year's Eve, not New Year's Day."

"And your point is?"

Chrissie rolls her eyes. "They left here after midnight. Unless they had sex in the supply closet, which I know for a fact they didn't, I won the bet."

Hailey's eyes narrow on her. "You can't be certain they didn't have sex in the supply closet."

Chrissie winks. "It was occupied."

"What about the office? There's a couch in there. It's much more comfortable than the supply closet."

"Um." Faith bites her lip and her cheeks darken.

Mary Ann sighs with a goofy smile on her face. "Have I mentioned how much I love this place yet today?"

"Easy for you to say," I bitch. "Everyone isn't staring at you asking when exactly you had sex last night."

She waves away my comment. "Oh, we didn't have sex last night."

Barney waggles his eyebrows. "Equipment not working for you, old man?"

Mary Ann smiles. "My shift didn't end until four this morning. We had sex an hour ago when Sid woke me up with his—"

"Na! Na! Na! Na! I can't hear you!" Phoebe shouts and covers her ears.

Suzie stands in front of her and yells, "They had sex this morning when—"

Phoebe slaps a hand over Suzie's mouth. "You're cruel."

"I withdraw my earlier statement. I love this place, too," I say as I watch Suzie try to peel Phoebe's fingers off of her mouth.

Hailey rubs her hands together. "Great. Now tell us when exactly the deed happened."

Before I can open my mouth and tell her it's none of her business, Faith grabs my hand and drags me down the hallway away from everyone.

She shoves me into the office, but before she can shut the door Hailey, Phoebe, Suzie, Chrissie, Lexi, and Mary Ann push their way in.

"You can't kick us out," Suzie declares. "It's in the rules."

"What rules?" I ask.

She shrugs. "I don't know, but it's what you say when you want to get your way."

"Whatever. What are we doing here?" I ask Faith.

"I'm rescuing you. You looked uncomfortable." She wrinkles her nose. "Which is weird. You usually don't have a problem talking about your sexcapades."

I blow out a breath of air and collapse on the sofa. "Because my sexcapades don't usually end with the man calling me another woman's name."

"What?" Hailey shrieks. "Barney doesn't have another woman. He hasn't been with a woman since I've known him."

"Do you need me to get the information from Wally?" Chrissie offers.

Hailey snorts. "As if Wally will talk."

"I can find out who she is from Max," Faith says.

"No, it's fine. I don't need to know who she is. The fact that he said her name during sex is enough for me."

I'm done with Barney Lewis. It's for the best. I don't do relationships and our friends are all intertwined. It would get messy. And I don't do messy any more than I do relationships.

Chapter 10

I want someone to look at me the way I look at chocolate cake.

"I have the perfect thing to cheer you up," Faith says when I open my apartment door to her a few days later.

"Who says I need cheering up?"

She points to my face. "The grumpy scowl on your face right this second."

I open my mouth to deny it – despite my grumpiness being obvious to everyone within a ten-mile radius – but Faith lifts a hand to stop me.

"I need someone to help me with wedding stuff today."

"Why didn't you say so in the first place?" I love wedding stuff. "Let me grab my purse."

"And your jacket. It's literally freezing out there."

"What are we doing?" I ask once we're in Faith's car driving toward downtown with the heat on full blast.

She smiles at me. "Cake testing."

"Awesome."

Who doesn't love cake? I should probably not love cake considering I'm a good twenty pounds overweight, but I don't give a rat's ass. Cake is yummy. Chocolate is the food of the gods. And I deserve it.

"Max didn't want to come?"

"Max wants to get married at the courthouse. He doesn't care about having a reception to celebrate our marriage."

I sigh. "The man loves you and can't wait to marry you. I'm beyond happy for you."

She clasps my hand. "Now to find you a man."

"Have you met me? I don't do long-term with a man."

She lets my hand go and grasps the steering wheel. "Yeah, I know. But I want you to be happy."

"I don't need a man to be happy." And I don't. Hell, I don't need a man to satisfy me either. There are tools for that.

We park in front of a bakery downtown, and I hop out of the car. "This place is adorable," I say as I scan the pink and white striped awning.

We enter the place and it's as cute on the inside as it is on the outside. The walls are pink and white striped and there are white bistro tables and chairs with pink cushions with hearts on them. Each table is set up for two people. Most of the tables are already occupied by couples. Faith points to a table near the window and we sit down.

A woman clears her throat to gain our attention. "Now that all of our couples have arrived, we can get started. I'm Sarah and I'll be hosting this cake tasting today. We'll begin with—"

Her words are cut off when the door bangs open and Chrissie, Hailey, Phoebe, and Suzie rush inside.

Suzie studies the tables. "Oh good. We're not too late."

Hailey and Chrissie drag another table to ours and find seats for everyone. The six of us end up squished around two tables.

"How did you find us?" Faith asks.

Chrissie grunts. "Don't insult me."

"I can't believe you thought you could go to a cake testing without me." Suzie widens her eyes and does her best to look upset.

"And you know how much I love cake," Phoebe

whines.

Hailey snorts. "What happened to the woman who existed on rabbit food when she first arrived in Milwaukee?"

"She became a fox," Phoebe answers.

"Pff." Suzie waves a hand in Phoebe's direction. "You always were a fox."

Sarah claps her hands from the front of the group. "It's lovely all of your friends are here to support your wedding, but could we begin now?"

"Actually," Chrissie says, "we're waiting for one more person."

Lexi rushes inside and scans the room. "What's going on? Where's the threat?"

Chrissie waves her over. "No threat. We're tasting wedding cake today."

Lexi's hand drops from her hip where I now notice a weapon is holstered. A weapon? Who is Lexi? Who is Chrissie for that matter? The two of them are 'work' friends. What type of work calls for two kickass women? Inquiring minds want to know.

"Can we get started now?" Sarah shouts.

Lexi motions for her to continue before scanning the room for a free chair. She finds one and drags it across the floor causing a loud scraping noise. Everyone in the room is staring at her with their mouths gaping open. She doesn't seem to notice them as she squeezes herself between Chrissie and Hailey.

"They're going to kick us out of here," Faith mutters.

Hailey snorts. "They're not going to kick us out. Have you seen the price of these cakes? If they want you to buy one of them, they'll put up with us all day and all night."

"We'll be starting with a vanilla cake with vanilla buttercream," Sarah announces as someone rolls out a cart containing plates with tiny cubes of cake.

Suzie pops the cake into her mouth. "Next!"

Faith hangs her head. "I'm going to need to find a new baker."

"Why?" I ask. "This place is awesome."

"Except for the drinks." Hailey's nose wrinkles at the water on the table. "I was hoping for champagne."

"I got you covered." Chrissie removes a bottle of champagne from her bag.

Faith's eyebrows nearly fly off her forehead. "You brought champagne?!"

"Duh. The website clearly indicated they don't serve alcohol here."

Hailey holds out her water glass. "I'm in."

Chrissie pops the champagne, and everyone turns to stare at us. Faith's cheeks darken until they're the color of tomatoes, but I smile and wave at everyone.

"Fill me up. I'm not driving." I shove my glass at Chrissie.

A man behind Chrissie clears his throat. "What do you want?" she asks him without bothering to look his way.

"Got enough champagne for me?"

"And me?" Another man whisper-shouts.

Chrissie holds up the bottle. "Let me fill up my girls first."

Sarah stomps over to our table. "What are you doing?" She hisses. "This is a cake testing."

"There isn't a whole lot of cake for it being a cake testing," Phoebe mumbles.

"I agree with Pheebs. The portion sizes are for midgets." Since Suzie is a midget at five-feet-two, you'd think she'd be okay with the portion sizes. You'd be wrong.

"Good thing you're a midget, then," Hailey points out as she sips her champagne.

"I'm sorry," Faith says before anyone can speak again. "We'll behave, I promise."

Sarah glares at the group of us. "You better," she orders before leaving.

"I never promised I'd behave," Lexi says as she picks up her champagne.

I clink my glass with hers. "Me either." I wink.

Faith's head falls to the table with a thunk. "Why me?"

I nudge her. "You love us, and you know it."

"More cake," Phoebe squeals as a waiter appears with another cart.

The man at the table behind us glances over and his eyes widen when his gaze lands on Phoebe. He doesn't bother to hide his interest as his gaze roves over her. Phoebe waves her left hand in his face. "Married." She points to her belly. "And pregnant."

The woman sitting next to him slams her hand down on the table. "Are you checking out another woman when we're at a cake tasting for our wedding?"

"Tell him, sistah!" Suzie shouts and punches her first in the air.

"I cannot believe you." The woman jumps to her feet causing her chair to tip over and clatter to the floor. She grabs her coat and marches out of the bakery. The man sits there with this dazed and confused expression on his face. Idiot.

"Go after her, you numbskull," I order him and for good measure, I kick his chair.

He sighs and gets to his feet before lumbering out of the café.

"Good," I say. "Now, we can spread out."

We spread ourselves out over three tables as the waiter distributes more cake samples.

"I get roving eye guy's cake," Phoebe says as she nabs an extra plate from the trolley.

"And I get the fiancée's cake," Suzie claims.

Lexi leans back in her chair and sips her

champagne. "You know you can buy some cake, right? We are in a bakery after all."

"Where's the fun in that?" Suzie asks.

"Speaking of fun, how much fun did you have with Lenny on New Year's Eve?" Hailey waggles her eyebrows.

Lexi cocks an eyebrow at Chrissie who shrugs. "Sorry. Not sorry. You're the one who decided to stick around."

"You could have at least warned me your friends are crazy."

"Crazy and proud of it." Suzie holds up her hand and I slap it.

"I have Valentine's Day," Hailey calls out.

"Valentine's Day for what?" Lexi asks.

Chrissie sighs. "They have a thing with betting on when relationships develop."

Hailey snorts. "Relationships develop? Um, no. We're betting on when Lenny gets your pants off."

"I think I made a mistake sticking around here."

Chrissie bumps her shoulder. "You'll love it here, don't worry."

"Maybe Max and I should elope. He doesn't want a wedding anyway," Faith mumbles.

"No way. You are not eloping. You are not denying me the chance to be your maid of honor while you marry the man you love. I let you marry idiot Silas and stood by you while he treated you like yesterday's smelly trash. I earned the maid of honor spot."

"Way to make my wedding about you, Valerie."

I wink at her. "As long as we understand each other."

Chapter 11

Why should you never marry a tennis player? Because love means nothing to them!

I have successfully avoided Barney the dirtbag for a week now, but my streak ends today. It's for a good cause, though. Max adopted Ollie today, and they're celebrating at the pub tonight. I am not missing my godson's adoption party for anything.

"Aunt Val, you made it!" Ollie shouts as he runs toward me.

I hug him up tight until he squirms to be released. "Congrats, kid." I ruffle his hair.

He scowls at me, "Knock it off."

I flourish the gift I bought him. "I guess you don't want this then?" I wink before handing it to him.

He tears the wrapping off the box. "A Garmin smartwatch. This is awesome! I can monitor my heart rate when I'm playing soccer. I made the varsity team this year."

"I know." Everyone in the city of Milwaukee knows. He hasn't stopped talking about it since the coach announced the line-up.

"Tell Aunt Valerie thank you," Faith orders.

"Thanks, Aunt Val."

I tap my cheek. Ollie rolls his eyes before bending over to kiss my cheek. "You're a nut."

"That's Aunt Nut to you," I shout as he rushes off.

Faith laces her arm with mine. "How are you doing?" she asks as she leads me to the bar where everyone has gathered to hang out.

"I'm fine. Tired, but fine. I'm starting to think Mr. Davenport is a vampire who doesn't need sleep."

"Vampires need sleep," Suzie chimes in. "And, since they can't go out in the sun, I doubt your boss is one."

Hailey sighs. "Vampires don't exist. Just like telepathy doesn't exist."

"Let's ask Chrissie." Suzie cups her hands in front of her mouth and yells across the room, "Chrissie."

Chrissie strolls over to us. "You rang?"

"Do vampires exist?"

She nods, and Suzie pumps her fist. "Yes!"

"Vampire bats are found in Central and South America. They feed solely on blood."

Suzie sticks her tongue out at her. "Not what I meant, and you know it."

"How did you manage to find Silas anyway?" I ask Faith since I'm done talking about vampires. I'm all for a vampire romance, but I know it's just a fantasy. "You needed to find him to complete the adoption procedure, didn't you?"

Faith shrugs. "Max found him."

Chrissie clears her throat. "Not to dis your husband, but I found Silas."

Wally kisses her hair. "No bragging, Angel."

She cocks an eyebrow at him. "You brag all the time, Bossy."

The door slams open and Barney stomps inside. He marches up to Wally. "Not funny, brother. Not funny."

"What's not funny?" Phoebe asks.

Barney points at Wally. "Someone ordered me a taxi for three o'clock this morning. When I told the driver there was a mistake, he said I told him I'd say that. I had to give him a twenty-dollar tip to get him to leave."

He does appear to be a bit sleep deprived. His normal three-day beard growth is unruly and there are circles under his eyes. Good. At least, I'm not living in sleep deprived land by myself. Unfortunately, my sleep deprivation was caused by the sexy jerk and not a prank.

Nope. Val. The sleep loss is your boss' fault, remember? I don't lie to myself very well.

Wally crosses his arms over his chest. "Serves you right. You know how much I hate clowns."

"Your wife initiated the clown prank. Did you get her back?"

"I most certainly did." Wally leers at Chrissie and she slaps his shoulder.

Suzie rubs her hands together. "Sid is the only one left. I can't wait."

"Can't wait for what?" Sid asks as he joins the group.

"For Wally to prank you."

Mary Ann frowns at her husband. "What did you do now?"

He kisses her hair. "Never you mind."

"He helped Chrissie prank Wally. Everyone in the bar dressed up like clowns and scared the daylights out of him," Suzie explains. "It was classic!"

"Coulrophobia is more common than people think. You should probably consult a mental health provider for assistance. I can give you a few names," Mary Ann offers.

Barney guffaws. "I love your wife, Sid."

Sid growls at him. "Stay away from my wife." He nods toward me. "You've got your own woman."

I hold my hands out in front of me as I retreat. "The hell, he does."

Barney steps toward me, but I glare at him to stop him. "Don't even think about it."

He stares at me for a moment, but I don't back down. Finally, he clears his throat and launches into one of his dirty jokes. "What's the best part about gardening?" He pauses for a second. "Getting down and dirty with your hoes."

He holds up his hand to Hailey for a high-five, but she crosses her arms over her chest. "Not funny, Uncle Barney. Not funny."

"I'm going to check if Carol needs help bringing out the cake," I say before making my escape.

Faith ordered a huge cake for Ollie from the bakery after the cake tasting last weekend. She felt guilty for how our party 'disrupted' the other couples and spent entirely too much money on a chocolate cake. There was no reason to feel guilty. Our 'disruption' involved Chrissie popping open a second bottle of champagne, which she shared with the other attendees. A good time was had by all.

Faith follows me into the kitchen. "Are you okay? Do you want me to have Max kick Barney's ass?"

"Can Max kick Barney's ass?"

Barney's leaner than Max, but I know from experience he's hiding a muscular body underneath his clothes. My breasts tingle when I remember all of the things his muscular body is capable of. *Stop it, Val.* No more thinking about our sexy times together. I slam the door on those memories.

"I have twenty on Pops," Hailey says.

"Have you considered seeing a mental health specialist yourself? For your gambling addiction?"

She sticks her tongue out at me. "Don't ruin my fun."

"My money's on Barney," Chrissie says, and I cock an eyebrow at her. "The skinny guys don't fight fair."

There's no doubt in my mind Barney wouldn't fight fair. Fair isn't a word in his vocabulary. For example, maybe he could have told me he's in love with someone named Ruby before he pushed me down on my sofa and had his way with me. So much for slamming the door on those memories.

"Do you want me to kick Barney's ass for you?"

Max asks as he strolls through the door.

I glare at Faith. Did she tell him what happened between me and Barney? "Do you tell him everything?"

She shrugs. "He's very persuasive."

"Are we having a party in the kitchen?" Phoebe asks. "Why didn't anyone tell me? Baby Rossi is hungry."

Carol slaps Phoebe's hand when she reaches for a drumstick. "There are vegetables in the refrigerator if you can't wait five minutes until I serve the food."

"Vegetables?" Phoebe feigns gagging.

"Why is everyone in the kitchen? Are you planning a surprise for me?" Ollie scans the room.

Faith places her hands on his shoulders and steers him toward the door. "No surprise. Dinner's ready. Go wash your hands."

"Ma," he complains.

"No whining."

"Dad?"

Max ruffles his hair. "Nice try, kid. Nice try. But you forget I raised a teenager already. The whining has no effect on me."

Yes, it does Hailey mouths to Ollie. They bump fists before he leaves. He doesn't go in the direction of the restroom and Faith sighs before following him. Max stops her. "I got it." He kisses her forehead before following his brand new adopted son.

Carol's had enough, which she makes abundantly clear when she orders, "If you're not cooking, you need to leave my kitchen."

She doesn't need to tell me twice. I skedaddle and make my way toward the restrooms to wash my hands. I don't make it there. Barney is leaning against the wall in the hallway. When he sees me, he pushes off from the wall to block the women's restroom.

"Val, can I talk to you?"

I glare at him. "What is it with you and talking? I

A Valentine for Valerie

didn't want to talk to you before we had sex, and I certainly don't want to talk to you now."

"I need to apologize."

"What you need to do is move so I can go to the restroom."

"Yeah, Barney. Leave our girl alone," Chrissie says as she comes up behind me. "Do you need me to get rid of him?"

"I'm fine."

"Yeah, but kicking him out on his ass sounds like fun."

Wally chuckles before grasping her shoulder and hauling her away. "No kicking my brother's ass."

"Why not?" She pouts. "He deserves it."

"I know, Angel. I know," Wally says, and I huff. Goodness gracious, you can't keep a secret with this crowd.

"Does everyone know Barney called me another woman's name during sex?" I shout.

Five women's heads peak around the corner of the hallway. "I know, so everyone else must know, too," Mary Ann says. "You should know none of the men around here can keep their mouths shut."

"Men?" I raise an eyebrow.

Carol enters the hallway with her hands full of food. "Clear out everyone. The hallway needs to be clear in case of a fire." She glances over her shoulder at me and winks.

I don't know Carol very well, but I owe her one for distracting Barney so I can sneak into the women's room. Avoiding the man is more difficult than I thought it would be.

Chapter 12

What did the astronaut's fiancée say when he proposed to her in open outer space? "I can't breathe!"

Barney

I've had enough of Valerie avoiding me. I know I screwed up in the worst way when I accidentally called her Ruby, but she needs to let me apologize properly. Then, we can move on.

She can't ignore me now. Not when I'm standing in the hallway outside her apartment. I knock and hear her walk to the door, but she doesn't open it or speak. I should have known.

"Come on, Val. I know you're home." I pause, but there's no response. "Your shadow is visible underneath the door."

At my words, the light from underneath her door dims. I chuckle. She doesn't seriously think she can get rid of me this easily, does she?

"Switching off the light kind of proves my point, doesn't it?"

I hear a soft huff.

"Come on, Trouble. Let me in."

The door down the hall opens, and an old lady sticks her head out.

"Do you want all your neighbors to hear what I have to say?"

"I don't want to talk to you." I don't need much of an imagination to know she's standing on the other side of the door with her arms crossed over her magnificent chest glaring daggers at me through the door.

"I want to talk to you."

"Too bad. You can't always get what you want."

"If you don't open this door, I'm going to say everything I need to say in the hallway where everyone can watch and listen."

"Go for it. The whole world already knows what happened anyway."

I grimace. Unfortunately, she's not wrong. You can't keep a secret between my brothers and their women. Add in Hailey and her friends and there's not a chance of a secret remaining private. Unless you happen to be Chrissie. No one wants to disclose her past and get on her or Wally's bad side.

"I need to apologize face to face."

"Buy a clue, Barney the dirtbag. I don't want to see your face. I thought I made this perfectly clear last night at the bar."

She certainly did. She avoided the hell out of me. My brothers found it hilarious. I won't be hearing the end of how *my* woman runs away from me after sex for a long ass time. No amount of explaining how Val is not *my* woman could shut them up.

"I'm not joking. I'll say what I have to say right here in the hallway. And I'm not alone out here."

I glance down the hallway and sure enough, the old lady is no longer peeking out of her doorway. She's now standing in the hallway not bothering to pretend to not listen.

"You can talk until you're blue in the face. I'm still not letting you in."

I place my hand on the door and lean in close to whisper, "I'm sorry, Val. There's no excuse for what I did."

"Damn right, there isn't."

I clear my throat. I don't want to tell her this and speaking through the door knowing there are other people listening doesn't make it any easier. "I don't usually relax with women after we've had relations."

"Had relations? We had sex, Barney. Sex. S.E.X. Come on, you can say the word." There's my trouble. Not afraid to come out and say it like it is.

I feel the old lady edging closer and closer to me.

"I'm trying not to broadcast our business to everyone in this building."

She laughs. "I'm not embarrassed we had sex. I'm a forty-five-year-old independent woman. I'll have sex if I want to, and I will not be shamed."

"And you shouldn't be. I didn't mean the sex part. I meant the part after."

"The part where you called me another woman's name, you mean?"

She can't help herself from throwing my mistake in my face, can she?

"Let me come in so I can apologize in person."

"Tell you what. I'll let you inside to apologize if you tell me who she is."

Damn. I should have known this was coming.

"I can't."

"Can't or won't?"

"It's complicated." I haven't told anyone about what happened with Ruby. My brothers know because they were there. I can't imagine telling Valerie how I failed my wife. She'd never forgive me then.

"We're done." She doesn't give me a chance to respond before she switches on her radio and increases the volume until the music is blaring.

I place my hand against the door. "We are not done," I whisper to it.

I stomp down the hallway, but before I reach the stairs, the old lady yells out to me. "I'd forgive you!"

I flick a hand in her direction before bounding down the stairs. I need a beer and the company of my brothers.

When I enter the pub thirty minutes later, Lenny

A Valentine for Valerie

takes one look at me before holding out his hand to Sid, "Pay up."

Sid slaps a ten-dollar bill in Lenny's hand. "I was convinced he'd manage to get her to forgive him," he mumbles.

Wally smirks. "If you need any pointers on getting your woman to forgive you, let me know."

"What are you doing here?" I ask. "Shouldn't you be at home cuddling up with your new wife?"

Sid laughs. "Chrissie kicked him out."

Wally shoves Sid's shoulder. "She didn't kick me out. She's studying and needed quiet in the house."

Max ambles over and sets a tray of beers on the table. "Give her time, brother. She'll come around."

"But I need to apologize."

"While you're naked in bed with her," Lenny says with a wiggle of his brows.

I grunt. "I'm not making Valerie my woman."

Max slaps my shoulder. "It's time to let your guilt go."

"You didn't do anything wrong," Wally adds.

I growl at them. "Yeah, I did. Ruby's dead because of me."

Lenny crosses his arms over his chest. "Who are you, God? You could no more prevent Ruby's death than you can the sun from setting."

"I could have. If I had paid attention, I—"

Max squeezes my shoulder to the point of pain. "Stop. We've let you wallow in your guilt for too damn long. It's been decades, brother."

"Since a woman has finally caught your eye, we're not letting your useless guilt carry on any longer," Sid adds.

"Caught my eye? No one's caught my eye."

Lenny snorts. "Yeah, right. Need we remind you how you slept with Max's woman's best friend."

"You didn't shit where you eat, brother," Sid adds.

I get it. I shouldn't have messed around with Val unless it was serious. Too bad I can't seem to keep my hands off of her.

"You're one to talk," I snarl at Sid. "How many wives have you had now? Six, seven?"

Sid doesn't fall for the bait. He leans back in the booth with a shit-eating grin on his face. "Mary Ann is number six and she was worth waiting for. The question is – is Valerie the one who's worth waiting for?"

"I haven't been waiting."

I haven't been in a relationship since Ruby died. It's not because I'm waiting for 'the one'. I'm done with relationships. I couldn't keep my first wife alive. I have no right to have a woman again after I couldn't save my first one.

"I'm thinking Valerie is the woman who's going to work your unwarranted guilt right out of you," Max says before strolling back to the bar.

"Like Faith did with you?" I shout after him.

"Brother, trust me, it's worth it."

"Are we done talking about feelings like a bunch of menopausal women?" I bark at my brothers. I down my beer and stand. "I'm going to play some pool."

My brothers don't let me escape. Of course, they don't. Since the topic of Ruby has been officially revived, I'm not going to hear the end of it from them until I let go of the guilt. I guess I'm never going to hear the end of it, then, because it's my fault my wife is dead. And no one can convince me otherwise.

Chapter 13

How did the telephone propose to its girlfriend? He gave her a ring.

"Holy Toledo. This place is fantastic," I say as Faith and I enter the hotel. There are marble floors and painted murals on the ceiling. Fancy doesn't cover it.

"I know. This is where Phoebe had her wedding reception." Faith bumps my hip. "By the way, it's Milwaukee, not Toledo."

Faith and I are here to check out a band for her wedding. The band is playing for a wedding tonight and the bridal pair agreed we could attend the reception.

"I thought you were having a small party at McGraw's. A band does not say small."

"I think I'm getting carried away." She screeches to a halt. "Am I getting carried away?"

"Who cares? You're marrying the man of your dreams. Get carried away. Have a big shindig. Go all out. After everything Silas put you through, you deserve it. Scratch that. You deserve it because you're a wonderful person regardless of what happened with Silas."

She smiles. "You're right. Let's go check out this band."

"I'm telling you right now. If they don't play music I can dance to, I'm vetoing."

"Is there music you can't dance to?"

We follow the directions to the ballroom. If I thought the entry to the hotel was fancy, I was wrong. Because the ballroom is the definition of fancy. The walls are covered in golden wallpaper, the floors are adorned with oak parquet, and there are crystal chandeliers dangling from the ceiling.

"I should have gotten out my ball gown for this."

Faith cocks an eyebrow. "Do you own a ball gown?"

"No," I say as I scan the room. "But I'd buy one if I had an event to wear it to."

I do love to get all dressed up. And I might own a few too many clothes. As in I transformed the second bedroom in my apartment into a closet.

"Oh good, the band hasn't started yet."

At Suzie's words, I whirl around to find Suzie, Hailey, Phoebe, Chrissie, and Lexi standing in the doorway.

"What are you doing here?" Faith hisses. "I told the bride I'd come with one person, not an entire football team."

Chrissie rolls her eyes. "We're seven people, not hardly a football team. Not even enough for a soccer team."

"Not my point and you know it."

Chrissie waves away Faith's concerns. "Don't worry about it. I already cleared our attendance with the wedding planner."

At her announcement, my eyes widen, and I study her. "Who are you, Chrissie Lindberg?" The woman is fascinating. I didn't know whose wedding this is, and she somehow found out who the wedding planner is and invited herself? Amazing.

She flashes her wedding rings at me. "It's Chrissie Nelson now."

Lexi purses her lips. "I can't believe you took a man's last name. Whatever happened to I am woman hear me roar?"

"I still roar. Don't you worry about it." Chrissie winks.

Phoebe frowns as she studies the room. "It figures. They don't have a buffet. I thought we'd get food."

"There's a bar in the lobby. I bet they serve food. Come on, mini-Grayson's hungry, too." Suzie threads her arm through Phoebe's, and they walk off.

Hailey rubs her hands together. "The pregnant women have left the building. Time to find out what fancy drinks rich people serve at weddings."

"You know Phoebe's rich," I point out. I don't know her story, but her clothes scream 'I come from more money than you will ever possess in a million lifetimes'. Like I said – I know clothes.

Hailey rolls her eyes. "Which is why I waited until she left to say anything."

"Come on. There's our table." Chrissie points to a table in the corner.

"We have a table?" Faith mutters as we walk there.

"Ooooh, there's champagne." Hailey pops the cork and pours us glasses. "Raise your glasses, ladies. To my pops finding love with a woman I actually don't hate."

Faith rolls her eyes before clinking her glass with Hailey's.

"I hope they don't do some elaborate dance thing for the bride and groom's first dance. They never dance as well as they think they do." Chrissie shivers.

"If they want to do a dance, let them do a dance." I pause. "You can always record it and put it on YouTube with suggestions for improvements."

"Good idea." She removes her phone from her purse.

Faith smacks the phone out of her hand. "No." Chrissie opens her mouth. "I said no."

"Now, I know why Suzie calls you her substitute mom," Chrissie whines.

Faith's eyes narrow, and Chrissie points at her before barking out a laugh. "Gotcha!"

The lights flicker before the band walks onto the stage. The guitar player begins to strum on his guitar as the bride and groom make their way to the dance floor. The groom is hanging off the bride who is obviously struggling to stay upright under his weight.

When the singer croons the first words of U2's *All I Want Is You,* I glance over at Faith to see a smile light up her face. U2 is one of her favorite bands. Ask me about the time she flashed a security guard in the hopes of getting backstage. She didn't get backstage, but she did get the guard's phone number. Too bad she met Silas soon afterwards and our fun ended there.

"Five bucks says the groom falls flat on his face," Chrissie whispers.

"Five bucks says he passes out," Lexi answers.

"I've got five bucks on him throwing up all over her dress," Hailey says.

Faith gasps. "Shame on you!"

Hailey shrugs in response. "It is what it is."

I ignore the betting and focus my attention on the couple. The poor bride is battling to keep her groom upright. He trips and steps on her dress. When she shoves him off of her, the sound of ripping is clear to hear.

"You ruined my dress!" she shouts as she pushes him away from her. He goes flying across the dance floor and runs smackdab into a table. He crashes to the ground and the table tips over and lands on top of him.

"Huh. I should have seen this coming," Chrissie says before standing and marching to the dance floor. I grab my purse and rush to follow her.

Chrissie grasps the bride's elbow and steers her toward the exit. I follow close behind her in an effort to hide her backside from the crowd. They've already seen her lingerie, but there's no need for her to parade around in it.

When we reach the restroom, Chrissie sets the bride in the attendant's chair.

"My wedding is ruined. My dress is ruined. My life

is ruined!" The bride wails.

"I can fix your dress." I can fix nearly everything. If I had my sewing machine, I could make the dress appear brand new. But there's no time for sewing machines right now.

"Chrissie, help her out of her dress."

Chrissie studies the bride. "Um, how? Give me an M-60 and I can field strip it, but this dress appears way more complicated." Lexi nods in agreement.

Faith elbows Chrissie and Lexi out of her way. "I got this."

Once Faith has the bride undressed, she hands me the dress. "Do your magic."

"This is going to take a while." Luckily, the rip is on the seam, so a fix isn't impossible. But doing these tiny stitches takes time.

"Did the party move to the bathroom?" Suzie says as she and Phoebe tromp inside.

"I think..." Phoebe's words cut off as she rushes to a stall. Seconds later the sound of her puking can be heard.

"Don't worry. She's pregnant, not drunk," Suzie announces. "I told you not to have the second helping of spicy wings!"

Suzie scans the room and notices the bride sitting in her underwear. "What's going on? Did you get your period during the first dance? Suzie to the rescue! I'm a wizard at getting stains out."

The bride sniffs. "The woman in the toilet throwing up isn't the only one pregnant."

Suzie rubs her belly. "She most certainly isn't."

Hailey elbows her. "She meant she's pregnant, dummy."

"Congrats! Welcome to the pregnant sisters." Suzie holds her hand up for a high-five.

The bride stares at her hand for a moment before

slapping it. "I wish Robert was as excited as some stranger in the restroom." She surveys the room as if she just realized she's surrounded by strangers. "Who are you people anyway?"

"We're here to check out the band. I'm getting married next month," Faith explains. "I'm Faith, by the way."

"Cara. Nice to meet you. And thanks for your help."

"You're letting us attend your wedding reception, it's the least we can do," I say as I cut the thread. I hold up the dress. "There. This ought to do."

"Assuming my idiot husband doesn't step on my gown again." Cara reaches out for the gown, but Faith places a hand on her arm to stop her.

"Do you not want to be married to him? We can smuggle you out of here and arrange an annulment."

Chrissie's ears perk up. "Lexi, you're on the front door. I've got the back."

Cara waves her hands in the air. "No, no, no. I'm pregnant, remember?"

"And you can raise a baby by yourself. I did," Faith says.

"My pops was a single father, and I turned out all right," Hailey adds.

"Come on. Either way, you can't go running around in your underwear." I hand Cara her dress. "It is pretty, though. We should buy a set of lingerie for Faith for her wedding."

Cara places her hand on Faith's arm. "Please, send me your address. It will be my thank you for helping me out tonight."

After we help her into her dress, she marches to the door but glances over her shoulder before opening it. "And book the band. They're the best in the business."

Phoebe exits the stall. "What did I miss?"

I throw an arm around her shoulder. "I'll fill you in

A Valentine for Valerie

on the dance floor."

Chapter 14

Love is not having to hold in your gas anymore.

When are you going to talk to Barney?

I glare at my computer before typing my reply to Faith.

We're at work. Shouldn't you be working?

I'm starting to think working with Faith at the same law firm isn't going to be as fun in Milwaukee as it was in Saint Louis.

As if I can't do two things at once.

The phone rings and I glare at it before I realize it's an outside call and not Faith trying to push me to talk to Barney. She knows he called me another woman's name – during sex no less! She wouldn't put up with Max calling her another woman's name, why should I put up with it from Barney? A man I'm not in a relationship with.

The phone rings again, and I snap out of my thoughts of Barney.

"Mr. Davenport's office. How may I help you?"

"Joseph Sturgess. Davenport now."

"I'm sorry. Mr. Davenport isn't in. Would you like to leave a message?" And can you maybe talk in full sentences?

"Appointment today."

Nope. No full sentences.

"Mr. Davenport's fully scheduled today. Perhaps I can squeeze you in tomorrow." I flip through Davenport's schedule knowing full well there's no space to add a client meeting anytime soon. He's in the middle of jury selection for an upcoming trial.

"Today."

"I can ask if Mr. Davenport can meet with you after hours," I suggest.

"Six p.m.," he says and hangs up.

I guess I'll be working late this evening. I don't attend client meetings, but Mr. Davenport makes me sit outside his office at my desk whenever he meets with clients. It's 'unseemly' for him not to have a secretary whenever he's in the office.

I'm used to working with pretentious attorneys. I have been a legal secretary for twenty some years now after all. But Mr. Davenport wins the pretentious crown from every attorney I've ever worked for before. I should have known better when I asked what the attorney I'd be working for was like and everyone in the human resources office froze with forced smiles on their faces.

I message my boss to inform him of the last minute appointment. His response? A laundry list of files I need to copy.

"You're welcome, asshole," I mutter as I stand to do his bidding.

We have an entire department devoted to copying files, but does Mr. Davenport allow me to use them? Of course not. Lord help us if it isn't *his* secretary doing all of his copying tasks. It doesn't matter if it distracts me from other jobs I should be doing or cause me to work late nights. Nope. Mr. Davenport gets what he wants. Have I mentioned he wins the pretentious crown?

At five minutes before six a tall, burly man lumbers my way. His broad nose is crooked and has a bump in the middle of it making it clear it's been broken a time or two in the past. He also has a scar through one eyebrow and across his cheek. I do not want to know how he got it.

Mr. Davenport's clients are usually wealthy. His hourly fee is not an amount most people can afford, but this man is obviously not one of his normal wealthy clients. He reminds me of a thug from one of those mobster movies, which I may be secretly obsessed with.

I stand and force a smile on my face. "Mr. Sturgess?" He grunts. "Mr. Davenport is ready for you. If you'll follow me."

I escort him into the office and wait as the two greet each other.

"Can I get you a drink? Coffee, tea, water?"

"Bourbon."

My gaze flits to Mr. Davenport. I don't usually provide clients with bourbon, but I know he has a fully stocked bar.

"Run down to the store and fetch a bottle."

Fetch a bottle? What am I? A dog? I don't snap at my boss, though. I may have a big mouth, but I'm not stupid.

"Right away, Mr. Davenport." I manage to keep my face blank as I say the words and back out of the room.

I snatch my coat and purse and stomp toward the elevator. The elevator is packed as everyone else is on their way home. There should be an express elevator for those of us who are forced to work late because our boss is an arrogant prick.

As soon as I'm outside, the cold wind from Lake Michigan hits me and I regret not bundling up with a scarf, hat, and mittens. I'm not used to these Wisconsin winters. Although, guessing by the way people shiver and hurry on their way, there's no getting used to this weather.

The good thing about Wisconsin? Liquor stores are not hard to find. There's one a block away from the office. I hurry as fast as I can while trying not to slide all over the place on the slippery ground. I need to hit the mall for a pair of stylish boots to wear at work because these pumps aren't cutting it in this weather.

I sigh in relief when I enter the warm store. I find a bottle of Pappy Van Winkle and stand in line to pay.

"Hard day at work, darling?" A man behind me in line slurs his question. "I got the thing to help you feel better if you get what I mean."

A Valentine for Valerie

I cock an eyebrow as I allow my gaze to roam over the man. He's at least sixty years old and he's not aging well. Not like a certain someone else I know who doesn't let his age show. Ugh! *Stop it, Valerie. You are not allowed to think about Barney anymore.*

I purse my lips. "Sorry, dude. I'd bet whatever you've got isn't enough for me."

The other people in line laugh and start ribbing the man. I don't pay any attention. It's my turn to pay and I need to get my butt back to the office pronto. By the time I return to the office, nearly half an hour has passed. I'll be hearing about my 'dithering' from Mr. Davenport tomorrow. At least he doesn't berate me in front of clients. Small miracles.

I set the bottle of bourbon down on my desk before placing my purse in a drawer and locking it. I shrug out of my coat and throw it over my chair before finger-combing my hair. All set, I pick up the bottle and walk toward Mr. Davenport's office.

I'm surprised the door is open. Before I can announce my presence, Sturgess speaks. "I'm going to kill him. I don't have a choice."

Whoa. Did he say, 'kill him'?

"Don't get caught."

Sturgess grunts. "Why do you think I'm here? I need your advice on how not to get caught."

I bite my tongue before I can gasp and make my presence known. It's not Mr. Davenport's job to assist his clients in committing a crime. He's supposed to advise them after the crime's been committed.

"Of course. What were you thinking?"

My eyes nearly bug out of my head. Mr. Davenport should be telling Sturgess to get lost, not helping him hide a future crime.

Whatever Mr. Davenport is doing, I don't want to hear any more of this. I have a feeling Joseph Sturgess is the kind of person who wouldn't appreciate someone overhearing his business, especially when the business is 'killing him'. I want no part in any of this.

I clear my throat before stomping toward the door as loud as I can to make certain they hear me before I enter the office. I don't bother to force a smile on my face. Let them think I'm grumpy from having to go out in the cold to buy a bottle of bourbon.

I place the bottle on Mr. Davenport's desk. "Will there be anything else?"

My boss doesn't bother to glance at me. "No. Go home."

"Have a nice evening."

I shut the door on my way out of the office. I stand by my desk for a few moments until my hands stop shaking. Once I've gotten myself under control, I grab my purse and jacket and leave as fast as I can without attracting any attention.

Once I'm in the parking garage, I break into a run and unlock my door remotely. When I reach my car, I fling the door open and scramble inside before slamming the door behind me. I hit the lock button and take deep breaths to calm myself.

Holy crap! Mr. Davenport is a bad guy. Barney was right about this defense attorney. I wonder what Barney would think I should do. Ugh! *Stop thinking about Barney, Val.* You got yourself into this mess, you'll get yourself out. Just like you always do.

But I don't know what I should do. Do I call the police? Hailey's husband, Aiden, is a police detective. He might be able to help. He'd also blab every detail to the rest of the gang. Barney will hear about it and use the situation as an excuse to bug me again. No thanks.

I could leave an anonymous tip. Milwaukee must have an anonymous tip line. No. That won't work. What am I going to say? If I admit I heard Davenport and Sturgess talking, the police will figure out who called in no time. Even an idiot would know the only person who could possibly overhear an attorney and his client is the legal secretary whose desk is right outside the lawyer's office. No anonymous tip line then.

Wait a minute. Wait a minute. *Slow your roll, Val.* I'm probably overreacting. After all, I don't technically know my boss is a bad guy. Yes, Joseph Sturgess asked him to help him not get caught committing a murder, but I don't know how he responded. For all I know, he's recording this conversation and will hand the recording off to the police.

Yes, that's probably what's happening. Mr. Davenport golfs with the District Attorney after all. I'm freaking out for nothing. Everything will be fine.

I'll talk to Mr. Davenport tomorrow and confirm, but I'm convinced he'll handle everything in the proper manner. After all, Mr. Davenport is the embodiment of proper.

Chapter 15

You're like my dentures. I can't smile without you.

Mr. Davenport is busy with jury selection for his upcoming trial the next day. I can hardly call him and ask him to confirm he's not a dirty lying scoundrel. In my experience, it's always better to accuse someone of being a dirty lying scoundrel in person.

Faith arrives in front of my desk carrying my coat. "Come on."

"Come on where? What's going on? And why do you have my coat?"

She throws the coat on my desk. "We're going to lunch."

"Can't we eat in the cafeteria? It's brutal out there."

It snowed and then rained and then snowed again last night. I'm worried Mother Nature is having hot flashes. If so, we're in for a rough ride for the next few years. The roads were treacherous driving in this morning. I left thirty minutes early and I was still fifteen minutes late this morning. Mr. Davenport would have lost his mind had he been here.

"We can't gossip in the cafeteria."

I narrow my eyes at her. "If you're going to bug me about Barney the whole time, you're wasting your time."

"I promise not to bug you about Barney." She crosses her heart. "The whole time."

My stomach rumbles and makes my decision for me. "Fine. But I don't have all day."

We exit the building to discover the sun is shining and the snow has melted. What in the world? "I thought I was going to die driving to work this morning and now spring has arrived. Mother Nature has lost her dang mind."

Faith threads her arm through mine. "You get used to it."

Whatever. We make our way to the little sandwich shop on the corner. We order our food at the counter before finding a booth in the back.

"Do you have any real gossip?"

Faith's eyes sparkle as she leans forward. "Actually, I do." She surveys the place before leaning close and whispering, "You won't believe who I saw making out in the coffee room."

When she pauses for dramatic effect, I prod her, "Tell me. Who?"

"Mr. O'Brian and Penny."

My mouth gapes open. "You're kidding." Mr. O'Brian is a founding partner at the firm and coming up on a million years old. Penny is a twenty-something who started working at the firm a few months before I arrived.

Faith feigns gagging. "It was wrong. Oh, so wrong. Penny could be his granddaughter."

"I think you mean great-granddaughter."

We gossip about who else is having an extra-marital affair at the office while we eat our soup and sandwiches. We're packing up to leave when Faith says, "You should talk to Barney."

Shit. I thought I got away with not hearing the B-word. "No thanks."

"Maybe there's a story behind this other woman."

I freeze at her words. "Max told you who she is."

Her cheeks flame and she hums while glancing away. "No, he didn't."

"You are the world's worst liar."

"I can lie if I want to."

My nose scrunches. "Then, you didn't want to lie?"

She huffs out a breath. "I can't tell you. Max would

kill me."

"You mean Max wouldn't tell you any secrets again."

Her shoulders slump. "That too."

"It's fine, Faith. I don't need to know Barney's secrets. I know enough." Now, I'm lying. But I'm better at it. Faith doesn't bat an eyelash.

"At least tell me you'll come to the pub tonight for Hailey's birthday party."

I grin. "I wouldn't miss your step-daughter's birthday party for anything."

She sticks her tongue out at me. "You're cruel."

When we arrive back at the office after lunch, Mr. Davenport has returned. Time to put on my big girl panties and talk to him about what I overheard yesterday.

I knock on the door and enter. "Mr. Davenport, can I speak to you?"

He doesn't bother glancing up from his computer. "Of course, Ms. Cook. I want to speak to you about last evening."

Phew. He's going to tell me what I overheard was a misunderstanding without me having to bring it up. What a relief.

"I know you had to leave the building to purchase the bottle of bourbon, but you were gone for nearly thirty minutes. This is unacceptable."

Unacceptable? Is he kidding me with this?

"I hurried as quickly as I could considering the weather."

I hate defending myself to anyone, but this man isn't anyone. He's my boss. And if I want to keep my job, I have to remain amicable and not scream and shout at him regardless of how much fun it would be.

He frowns. "Ah, yes, I forget you're not from Wisconsin. I suppose I can let it go this one time."

I dig my nails into my palms to stop myself from

telling him exactly what I think of his response. "I need to talk to you about your client, Joseph Sturgess."

His hands lift from the keyboard. I've got his attention now. "What is it?"

"I accidentally overheard some of your conversation."

His lips purse. "Our conversation is protected under attorney-client privilege."

"Obviously. It's just …"

He grunts. "Just what?"

I glance behind me to ensure the door is shut tight before I speak. "It sounded like you were going to help him plan a murder."

He leans back in his chair. "Ms. Cook. Do you have any idea what my job entails?"

"You're a defense attorney."

"Which means I help clients who have been accused of crimes."

I barely manage to stop from rolling my eyes. Does he think I'm an idiot?

"But it sounded like Mr. Sturgess was planning a crime and not like he'd been accused of one."

"Are you seriously lecturing me on what my job is?" He sneers.

"No. I wouldn't dare. But attorney-client privilege doesn't apply if the attorney is assisting in the furtherance of a crime."

Mr. Davenport stands and places his hands on his desk before leaning forward to glare at me. "How dare you lecture me about the law? You're a secretary. I spent three years studying the law and twenty years since then practicing law. Who the hell do you think you are?"

I'm someone who's spent more than two decades working for criminal defense attorneys is who I am. I also hold an associate's degree in legal studies. I'm not some idiot who walked in off the street.

"It makes sense now," Mr. Davenport says.

Dare I ask what he's talking about? Hell yeah, I do. I'm not afraid of my boss.

"What does?"

"Why you were fired from your position in Saint Louis."

My stomach cramps at his reminder of Saint Louis. I know I did the right thing, calling out the lawyer for his blatant racism and sexism. Could I have acted with a bit more discretion? Yes, I could have. But discretion doesn't work when dealing with a racist, sexist asshole. At least not in my experience.

I bite my tongue. Mr. Davenport isn't the type of man who understands a woman who fights for justice. He probably thinks calling me a woman's libber is a slur. He'd be wrong.

"Nothing to say?"

He's egging me on. He wants me to lose my temper and shout the roof down. Why? What's his agenda?

I clear my throat. "Saint Louis was a regrettable situation." I have to force the words out of my mouth. I don't regret a word I said or how I said them. In fact, I don't regret many things in my life.

He stares at me for a long moment. I don't squirm as he scrutinizes me. I have nothing to squirm about.

"You're mistaken on what you heard last night. Mr. Sturgess is not planning a crime of any sort."

Holy crap. Mr. Davenport lied to my face. I know what I heard. It's not difficult to misinterpret the words *I'm going to kill him.*

"In any event, it will do you well to remember everything that happens within this office falls under the confidentiality clause in your employment contract."

In other words, I better keep my mouth shut or face being fired again. My heart rate increases, and I can feel a bead of sweat form on my brow. I do my best to keep my composure as I tell my boss, "I understand."

He sits again and returns his attention to his computer. "If there's nothing else…"

I don't bother responding. He wouldn't hear me now anyway. I back out of the office and close the door behind me.

I force myself to walk at a normal pace as I head toward the restroom. I lock myself inside a stall before sliding to the floor. I rub my hand over my chest as I attempt to get my erratic heartbeat under control.

Holy cow. Mr. Davenport is a bad guy. What am I going to do?

Chapter 16

What did the patient with the broken leg say to the doctor?
I have a crutch on you.

As soon as I enter McGraw's that night, Hailey snatches my hand and tugs me away from the door. She drags me to the bar where Suzie is sitting sipping a Shirley Temple while Grayson stands guard behind her to catch her if – more like when – she falls off. If you search for klutz in the dictionary, you'll find a picture of Suzie.

"What's going on?" I ask.

"Wally's up to no good," Hailey answers with a wide smile on her face.

"Do I want to know?"

Hailey's uncles are serious about their practical jokes. I hope none of them ever think they need to get revenge on me. I've reached the age where peeing yourself in fright is no longer merely a saying.

And Barney's the worst. If he's not doing practical jokes, he's telling dirty jokes. I love dirty jokes. It's what attracted me to Barney from the beginning. *No, Val. We're no longer attracted to Barney, remember?*

Hailey rubs her hands together. "I can't wait." She's a nut. I love her.

"Happy birthday!" I tell her before handing her a card.

I had no idea what to buy her, so I went with a gift card. But not a gift card to the mall or some other 'normal' store. Unlike myself, Hailey is not a girl who enjoys shopping at the mall. I don't think she knows the word fashion. She wears jeans and shitkicker boots no matter the time of year and the weather outside.

She opens the card and squeals when she sees the gift card to the shooting range. "Awesome!" She throws her arms around me. "Thank you, Aunt Val."

Aunt Val. When did I become Aunt Val? One, I'm not old enough to be her aunt. Unless I had a baby when I was twelve. I was still wearing a training bra when I was twelve. And why is it called a training bra anyway? What exactly is it supposed to be training? My breasts to grow bigger or me to get used to how uncomfortable bras are going to be for the rest of my life?

I cock an eyebrow at her. "Aunt Val?"

She shrugs. "It's only a matter of time before you succumb to Uncle Barney's charms."

What is it with people today and pushing me toward Barney? They all know what happened. "Did you miss the part about him calling me another woman's name in bed?"

She waves away my argument. "I bet he has his reasons."

"Besides," Suzie says as she motions to Barney who's strolling toward us. "He's a stone-cold fox." Grayson growls. She pats his chest. "Don't worry. No one's sexier than my baby daddy."

"Why does Dr. Pepper come in a bottle?" Barney asks when he's within hearing range.

I start to leave but then stop myself. Valerie Cook does not run from anyone, let alone a man.

"Because his wife died!" Barney shouts and holds his hand up for a high-five.

Suzie starts to raise her hand but pauses with it half-hanging in the air. "I don't think death is funny."

Grayson kisses her hair. "It's okay, precious. I'm over it."

I don't know their whole story, but apparently, when the two met, Grayson was in a deep depression over the death of his friend while they were stationed overseas.

Suzie did what she always does. She stuck her nose in and somehow Grayson fell in love with her instead of slapping her. It's a miracle.

"Lame," I declare to Barney to cover how jealous I am at Suzie and Grayson gazing at each other with hearts in their eyes. I don't do relationships for a reason I remind myself.

Barney crosses his arms over his chest. "As if you can do better."

Damn straight. I can do better. "What do you call the useless piece of skin on a dick?"

Suzie's hand flies into the air. "I know. Foreskin."

"No, the man."

Her eyes widen before she points at Barney. "Oh, burn."

Barney frowns. He opens his mouth to speak, but Hailey shushes him. "It's time. Sid's here."

The door to the pub opens and a bucket on top of the door tilts sending an entire nest of snakes down onto Sid and Mary Ann. Sid's scream is high-pitched as he bats the snakes away. "Get them off me! Get them off me!"

Mary Ann picks up one of the snakes and shoves it into his face. "They're fake, dummy."

His head recoils and hits the door with a loud thump. "Don't care. Put it down."

She wiggles the thing in his face. "How did I not know you're terrified of snakes? This is valuable information."

Sid gulps. "You can't use my fears against me."

"Why not?"

"Because it's in our vows."

She pats his chest. "You poor dear man. You don't understand the first thing about marriage," she says. She throws the rubber snake on the ground and struts away. Sid hurries to follow her.

They join Wally and Chrissie who are standing at a

A Valentine for Valerie

high-top table near us. Wally's smirking and Chrissie is giggling outright.

Sid snarls at Wally. "What the hell, man? You shouldn't use a man's fears against him."

Wally's smirk drops from his face and he crosses his arms over his chest. "Like you didn't use my fear of clowns against me."

Mary Ann sidles up to me. "This place is awesome. I need to get on the day shift. Speaking of work, how are you settling into your new job?"

At the thought of my job, my heart races again. I'm torn about what to do about what I overheard. I can't believe Mr. Davenport deals with scumbags like Sturgess. But he isn't seriously helping the man commit murder, is he? Maybe I'm blowing this all up in my mind. It's probably nothing.

Mary Ann squeezes my hand. "Where did you go? Are you okay?"

I force a smile on my face. "Sorry. You said work and my mind automatically went to the to-do list on my desk."

"Her boss, Mr. Davenport, is a dick," Faith says as she comes up behind me.

I snort. "What defense attorney isn't a dick?"

"I told you working for a defense attorney was a bad idea," Barney says.

"I'm confused. What possible business of yours could it be who I'm working for?"

He glares at me. "It is my business. You're—"

I shove my hand in his face. "I'm going to cut you off right there because you're obviously confused. Let me clear things up for you. I'm none of your business. None. Nod if you understand."

He crosses his arms and glowers at me. What he doesn't do is nod.

"Let me demonstrate. A nod is like this." I nod and watch as his face turns red. This is too much fun. I need to tease the man more often instead of running away from him.

Suzie claps. "This is awesome. I am loving being a witness to the uncles fall in love."

I snort. Love? Barney and I barely know each other. In fact, the man can't remember my name. At least not when it matters the most.

"I think you're confused," I tell her.

To my surprise, Barney doesn't back me up. He's too busy staring at me as if I'm a puzzle he can't figure out. Too bad for him my puzzle is closed to him for further inspection.

The lights dim and I freeze. Did we lose electricity? Uh oh. It's freezing outside. Literally freezing.

When the kitchen door swings open and Max exits carrying a cake lit up with candles, I sigh in relief. The candles cast enough light to see by, and I notice Barney is now positioned behind me.

My nerve endings stand at attention at his close proximity. I can feel his breath on my skin, and I shiver at the memory of how good his body feels when his heat is surrounding me completely.

My body sways toward him, but I lock my knees. I am not a slave to my body's desires. I elbow Barney instead. "You're crowding me."

"Sorry. You looked scared."

"Scared? I wasn't scared of a little blackout. And how could you tell I looked scared? It was too dark."

He shrugs. "I just can."

I push him away. My fingers tingle at the feel of his strong muscles underneath them. I snatch my hands away before I do something incredibly stupid such as caress his chest in front of everyone. I spin away and join the others in singing happy birthday to Hailey.

Hailey blows out her candles in one go. Suzie claps. "Good job. I thought you might have a tough time considering how many candles there are."

"You're the same age as me, numbskull."

"Nuh-uh. My birthday's months away."

"I get a corner piece," Ollie shouts.

"The birthday girl gets the first piece," Faith explains to him.

"There are four corners. If one is for Hailey, that leaves three corners left over."

Hailey wraps her arm around his neck and gives him a noogie. "You want a corner piece, brother? You have to ask nicely."

He tries to shove her away, but Hailey's no pushover. She may be thin, but she's five-foot-eight and learned to fight from her uncles.

"Fine!" he shouts and taps her shoulder. "I give in. May I please have a corner piece?"

She drops her arms. "Of course, little brother."

I smile at their antics. I wish I had a little brother. Then again, I wouldn't want anyone to endure what I did growing up. I shove thoughts of my mom and all my stepdads into the box where they belong. The box is covered in dust since I never open it.

"I want a corner, too!" I shout and dive into a discussion with Ollie about which flavor of frosting is the best. It's chocolate. There's no discussion to be had. But joking around with my godson is the best way to keep thoughts of my own 'family' at bay.

Chapter 17

What did one volcano say to the other volcano? I lava you.

I stumble as I climb the stairs in my apartment building. "Happy birthday to me. Happy birthday to me," I sing despite my birthday being months away.

I blame Hailey. The woman is addicted to tequila shots. I stuck to two shots, but it was enough for me to leave my car at the bar and grab a taxi home. I had to sneak out, though, since Barney had declared for anyone and everyone to hear how he would be driving me home. Yeah, right. Not happening.

I twirl my keys as I dance down the hallway toward my apartment. "Happy birthday to me. Happy birthday to me."

My keys fly out of my hands and land in front of my door. Oopsie. I kneel down to pick them up and realize my door is standing ajar. Huh. Weird. I know I closed and locked it when I left. I'm a single woman living on my own and have been for a long time. I know how important personal security is.

I nudge the door and it creaks open. I listen for a second, but I don't hear anyone inside. I stand to hit the lights and gasp when I see the state of my apartment. What the hell? Someone ransacked my place.

I grab the phone and dial Barney's number before I can think better of it. He picks up after the first ring. "Val? Are you okay?"

"Someone broke into my apartment," I whisper.

"Where are you? Get somewhere safe."

"They're gone." At least, I hope they are.

He growls. "Until I've checked for myself, I want you somewhere safe. Go to the nosy neighbor's apartment. I'll come find you there once I clear your place."

He hangs up before I have a chance to tell him he's overreacting. I scan the room. My television is in pieces on the floor. My sofa is completely shredded with the stuffing spread on the floor. And then there's the kitchen. The cabinets are hanging open and it looks as if the contents have been smashed on the floor. Maybe he's not overreacting. Time to get out of here.

I rush down the hallway and knock on my neighbor's door. She answers within seconds.

"There's been in a break-in," I say without greeting her.

She ushers me inside. "We need to call the police."

"Already done. They told me to find somewhere safe to wait for them." I don't know why I lie, but I can't think straight right now.

"Let me make you cup a tea."

She indicates her sofa for me to sit on, but I don't want to be alone and follow her into her kitchen.

"I'm Valerie by the way."

"Blanche," she says with a smile. "How do you drink your tea?"

I hate tea. But how the taste of tea makes me want to gag is the least of my worries at the moment. "With milk and sugar, please."

I sit at the dining room table and stare at the clock as I wait for Barney to arrive. Blanche attempts several conversations with me, but I can only stare at the stupid clock ticking the seconds away. What's taking this long? After fifteen minutes, there's a knock on the door and I jump to my feet. Blanche rushes to answer the door, but I'm hot on her heels.

"It's your male suitor," she calls when she opens the door to Barney.

Barney holds out his hand to me, and I don't hesitate to grasp it. He draws me close and wraps his arms around me before guiding me into the hallway and back to my apartment.

"You're safe," he murmurs into my hair as he rocks me back and forth.

I realize I'm trembling. *Get it together, Val.* Nothing happened. You weren't here when whoever it was decided destroying your apartment would make for a fun Friday night excursion.

"Hey, Aiden."

At Barney's greeting, I lift my head to find Hailey's husband standing in my living room. "What are you doing here?"

"I called him."

"Why?"

"Because someone broke into your apartment and destroyed your belongings. The last time I checked breaking and entering was still a crime, and Aiden's a police officer."

"But if Aiden knows then he'll tell Hailey and Hailey can't keep a secret to save her life."

At my words, his arms spasm. "Is there a reason you don't want Hailey knowing?"

"Besides everyone gossiping about my business? No."

He studies my face for a long moment. "You positive you don't have some secret and it's come back to haunt you?"

I scrunch my nose up. "What kind of secret? I'm batwoman on the lam?"

He flicks my nose. "Don't be flippant." His arm sweeps out to indicate the mess. "A secret that would lead to this happening."

"I have no idea why this happened." I haven't pissed anyone off as far as I know. Except my boss, but the man is Mr. Grumpy personified. Too bad he isn't

A Valentine for Valerie

handsome and misunderstood like those romance novels would have you believe all grumpy bosses are.

Aiden clears his throat. "I'll need you to make a statement, but we can do it tomorrow down at the station. In the meantime, pack a bag. You can stay with me and Hailey."

"I can stay here. This is where I live."

Barney growls. "You're not staying here. You're in danger here. What if this person comes back?"

"I'm not in danger. Someone broke into my place while I wasn't here. It happens. It sucks, but it happens."

He squeezes my neck before leaning down to look me in the eye. "This is not some random act. Burglars do not destroy houses. They certainly don't destroy televisions and coffee makers they can sell on the street for cash."

Oh no. Is he right? But why would I be targeted? Think, Valerie, think. This can't... No, it's not possible ... Could Joseph Sturgess possibly be to blame for this? But why would he target me? He can't possibly know I overheard him saying he's going to kill someone. I doubt he knows my name, let alone where I live.

"I don't know what to say." I'm not lying. "I don't know why anyone would target me."

It's only a teeny tiny white lie. After all, I can't be certain Sturgess is involved. It doesn't make sense for him to be involved after all.

"I'll give you this play tonight, honey. But tomorrow, we're talking."

I scowl. "Good luck with your delusion."

"Now, go pack a bag. You're staying with me."

"I'll pack a bag, but I'm not staying with you. What would Ruby think?"

Pain flashes in his eyes, but I ignore it. I can't be held responsible if I hurt him by mentioning Ruby since I haven't the first clue who she is and someone's not talking.

"I'll stay with Hailey and Aiden," I announce before

stomping off.

When I open my bedroom door, I have to clap a hand over my mouth to stop myself from screaming. What asshole did this? The blankets have been thrown off the bed to allow someone to stab the mattress. Plus, all the drawers of my dresser are open, and my clothes are strewn throughout the room.

I tiptoe around the mess to my closet. I say a little prayer to the goddess of fashion before sliding the door open. My wardrobe – all the gorgeous clothes I've spent my life collecting and maintaining – has been ruined. I fall to my knees to paw through the piles of fabric on the floor, but it's useless. Everything is in pieces. Someone took a scissor to all of my garments.

"Fuck!" Barney swears as he comes up behind me. He lifts me up and sets me on my feet. "Forget it. We'll buy you new clothes."

"Do you have any idea how long it took me to build this wardrobe?" I shout at him and promptly burst into tears.

He swears again before wrapping me up in his arms. "I'm sorry, honey."

His hands smooth up and down my back until my tears slow. Once I've collected myself, I push him away. He doesn't leave me alone. Of course not. He grasps my hand and leads me out of the bedroom into the living room. The empty living room.

"Where's Aiden?"

"He went home."

"Are you driving me to his house, then?"

"No," he grunts. "You're staying with me."

"I'm too tired and emotionally worn out to argue with you, but I'm officially lodging a complaint about this action."

He chuckles. "Complaint received."

He places a hand on my lower back and leads me out of the apartment and the building to his truck. We drive fifteen minutes until we're in the older historic district where we park in front of a warehouse.

"Is this the part where you confess you're a serial murderer? I have to warn you my skin is thin and wouldn't make a very good lampshade."

He opens my door and helps me out of the truck. Since I'm height challenged at five-foot-four and this truck is jacked up, I don't bitch at him about how I can get out of the truck on my own.

"This is where I live," he says as he leads me into the building. I notice there are several mailboxes in the foyer with names on them. Not a warehouse then.

When he opens the door to his place, I gasp. This is not the kind of home I expected Barney the jokester to live in. It's a studio loft with an industrial vibe to it. The ducts are visible on the ceiling and painted black. Since it's a studio, the bed is visible in the far corner of the room.

"Where am I supposed to sleep?" I ask.

Barney drops my hand to march to his dresser. He removes a t-shirt and flings it at me. "Here. To sleep in. We'll go to the mall tomorrow to buy you some clothes."

"You? You're going to the mall?"

He shrugs. "I'm fifty-seven years old. I've survived a shit ton of worse things than a trip to the mall."

I swallow. Way to stick your foot in your mouth, Val. This man is a veteran, remember? "I'm sorry. I didn't mean to be insensitive."

"You can have the bed. I'll sleep on the sofa. Bathroom's through there." He points to a door near the bed.

I scurry to the bathroom and lock the door behind me before stripping out of my clothes and putting Barney's t-shirt on. It smells like him. A fresh summer breeze and male musk. I lift the material to my face and inhale. The mere smell causes all my nerve endings to light up.

I release the t-shirt and let it fall around me. I'm not Ruby. Whoever she is. And I'd be smart to remember that.

When I exit the bathroom, Barney's camped out on the sofa with the television on and the volume down low. The corner of one side of the bed is turned down and there's a bottle of water on the bedstand. Barney's considerate. And kind of romantic. Who knew?

"Good night," I say. I hope sleep will sweep me away with its sweet oblivion because tomorrow is going to be one hell of a day between dealing with my apartment and the police. Not to mention some creep was in my place pawing through my things. Nope. I slam the gate on those thoughts.

Chapter 18

If kisses were snowflakes, I'd send you a blizzard.

Barney

I feel Valerie squirm in my arms, and I know she's finally waking up. She tossed and turned for hours last night before I gave up and climbed into bed with her. As soon as I wrapped my arms around her, she fell into a deep sleep. She won't thank me for sleeping with her, though. Too bad for her I don't care.

She freezes. She must have realized where she is. This is going to be fun.

"Good morning, Trouble," I whisper.

She scrambles out of my arms and I let her. She sits up against the headboard and glares down at me. The t-shirt I leant her last night is bunched up around her waist offering me a view of her creamy thighs and her sexy lace underwear.

"Stop staring at me like I'm a gazelle and you're a hungry lion," she hisses and pulls down the t-shirt. Since she's a tiny thing, the fabric covers her legs down to her knees. Damn. I was enjoying the view.

I knife up. "Are you hungry? I can make eggs and bacon." I start in the direction of the kitchen.

"You're going to walk off without talking about it?"

I stop. "Talking about what?"

Her mouth opens to speak, but her gaze drops to my chest and she gulps. I can't help the smirk from forming on my lips. She's focusing on my chest like she wants to take a bite. She's welcome to take a bite anytime she wants.

"Spot something you want?"

She rips her gaze from my body to my face. "No."

She's obviously lying, but I don't call her on it. "Eggs and bacon okay for breakfast?"

"Stop distracting me!"

"What do you want to talk about?" I ask because I know better than to tell her the truth – I'll never stop distracting her.

"You slept in bed with me. You said you'd sleep on the couch. Not cool, dude. Not cool."

I stalk toward the bed until I'm looming over her. "You were tossing and turning. If you think I'm going to let you miss out on a night of sleep after the day you had yesterday, you're wrong. Besides, the minute I climbed into bed with you, you settled and fell into a deep sleep."

Her eyes narrow into slits. "You had to ruin it, didn't you?"

I bend closer until I can feel her breath on my cheek. "I'm not going to apologize for enjoying having you in my arms all night."

She pushes me away, and I let her. "What would Ruby think about us sleeping in the same bed together?" She holds up her hand before I can speak. "No, don't answer. Kindly move out of my way. I need to get dressed and get home."

I don't move. "Get home? You're not going back to your apartment."

"Dude, you are not the boss of me."

In this, I sure as hell am. "I'm not letting you go back to your destroyed apartment. We don't know if it's safe."

And I know damn well and good she's hiding information from me. No one spends the time to utterly destroy an apartment and its belongings unless they're sending a message to the owner. The question is – what message is being sent? And who sent it?

"Let me?" she shrieks before scrambling off the

bed to get in my face. "No man lets me do anything. I'm my own woman and I'll do whatever I want whenever I want."

I scrub a hand down my face. "I'm not trying to boss you around. I'm trying to keep you safe."

She throws her hands in the air. "Why do you care? You don't want me for more than a roll in the hay. It's not your duty to keep me safe."

I growl before prowling toward her. She retreats until her back hits the wall. I slam my hands on the wall next to her head to cage her in. "You don't think I want you for more than sex? You're fucking wrong. I want you more than my next breath."

Her chest heaves with her choppy breaths. The feel of her soft breasts pressing against my chest is too much for me. I slam my lips on hers. She gasps, and I thrust my tongue into her mouth to explore.

This is not a gentle kiss. I don't have gentle in me right now. Not with Valerie being in danger. I thread my fingers through her hair and tug her head until it's angled just the way I need it. And then I plunder.

Valerie doesn't fight me. No, not my firecracker. She digs her fingers into my shoulders and draws me near until there's not an inch of space between the two of us. I roll my hips and rock my hard cock into her middle. She moans and hitches her leg over my hip. I throw her leg over the crook of my elbow opening her up to me.

I tear my mouth away from her soft lips to nip and bite my way down her neck until I reach her shoulder. My t-shirt hangs off of it allowing me access to her smooth skin. When I bite down on her shoulder, she groans and thrusts herself at me until she's withering against me.

"That's it, honey," I murmur against her skin. "Take what you need from me."

My phone blares with an incoming call. I ignore it, but Valerie freezes.

"Get off of me." She shoves against my shoulders. I release her leg and step back.

"This was a mistake."

I grit my teeth. "It was not a mistake."

She crosses her arms over her chest. "Are you forgetting about Ruby again?"

I grasp the ends of my hair and yank until the pain becomes unbearable. Fuck. I need to tell her about Ruby. And, once I've told her, she'll know how I didn't protect my wife. She'll run a mile in the other direction.

"Forget I asked. I need to shower and get dressed and then I'm going to my apartment to start cleaning up."

The hell she is. I point to the sofa. "Sit your ass down."

"Dude, how many times do I have to tell you I don't follow orders from any man?"

My nostrils flare as I force myself to take a breath before I pick her up and throw her on the sofa my damn self. An act I know won't earn me any favors with her.

"Will you please sit down?"

She stares at me for a long moment before finally nodding and sitting on the edge of the sofa. She pulls my t-shirt over her knees to cover herself. Her stance is defensive, and I don't like it one bit. She should never need to be uncomfortable around me. I grab the comforter off the bed and cover her with it.

I pace in front of her as I figure out how to begin. But there's no good place to begin.

"Ruby was my wife."

She gasps, and I hold up my hand.

"Please, let me get this out. I've never told anyone this before."

She slams her mouth shut and motions for me to proceed.

"Ruby and I married straight out of high school. She was my high school sweetheart. I joined the army right after we married. I had no interest in college and, besides, I wanted to start earning money immediately to provide for my Ruby."

I swallow. My Ruby. How long has it been since she was mine? I clear my throat. I can't let myself get bogged down in the past or I'll never get the words out.

"Everything was great to start with. Ruby never had any problem with me being gone for long periods of time. She was the first of the military wives to organize activities to keep the women's spirits up while we were gone."

I pause and blow out a breath. Now comes the hard part.

"But after we'd been married for two years, she started to change. I was away on a mission and whenever I called her, she'd bitch and rant at me for not being home with her. She was angry and resentful of me. I called less and less often. When I finally got home from the mission, she wasn't waiting for me with the other wives. I had to hitch a ride home from a buddy.

Ruby was there – sprawled out on the sofa. I was pissed. She hadn't bothered to come to the airport to await my arrival. And she laid into me the second the door shut behind me. How dare I leave her alone all the time? Was this what she could expect for the rest of her life?"

I pause. I've never told anyone this next part. Not even my brothers know. But I have to tell Valerie. If I want a chance with her – and after my heart stopped last night when I discovered she's in some kind of danger, I know I do want a chance with her – she needs to know it all.

"She hit me." I hear Valerie gasp, but I keep my gaze focused on the floor. "She balled her fists up and hit me over and over again. I let her. I figured I deserved it for deserting her. I promised I'd transfer to a different division. One where I wasn't out on missions all the time. But I couldn't transfer right away. I had one more mission first."

I rub my chest, but it doesn't erase any of the pain. Nothing ever will.

"We fought the entire time I was home. I could barely stand to be around her. I spent more and more of my time at the bar with my brothers. They didn't question me, but they knew things at home were rough."

Valerie wraps her arms around me from behind and I cling to her hands.

"I went out on another mission and when I came home Ruby was gone."

"Gone?" Val asks.

I clear my throat and force the word out of my mouth, "Dead. She had a massive brain tumor." My chin falls to my chest. "I failed her."

Valerie drops her arms and shoves on my shoulder. "Are you kidding me?"

What the hell? I bared my soul to this woman, and she responds with a snarl?

"You are not to blame for your wife's death. A brain tumor is."

She doesn't understand. "If I had realized why she was being aggressive, the doctors could have caught the tumor earlier. Instead, I thought she was being a bitch and I avoided her."

She fists her hands at her hips. "And what did the doctors say? Did they say she would have lived had they discovered the brain tumor earlier?"

I frown.

"They didn't. It's written all over your face. But somehow the big bad Barney thinks he knows more than modern medicine. You're an idiot."

I growl. "You're wrong. The doctors are wrong. If I had paid closer attention, I would have known she was sick. I could have saved her."

She throws her hands in the air. "Now you're God and can choose who lives and dies." I open my mouth to defend myself, but her hand covers it.

"No. Now, you listen to me, Barney Lewis. You are not responsible for your wife's death. Do you hear me?" She glares at me until I nod. "I know you don't believe me, but I'll say those words every day of my life until you do."

A Valentine for Valerie

I'm done talking about me and my failures. Valerie knows now. It's her choice what she does with the information. Now, it's time to find out what's going on with her.

"I gave you real. Now, it's your turn."

Her face pales, and I know I'm right. She is hiding something. Something dangerous. Her keeping secrets ends today. Because I will not fail to protect my woman this time. And make no doubt about it, Valerie is my woman. She has been since she winked up at me on Thanksgiving.

It's taken me a while to admit who this woman is to me, but I'm ready now. She's mine.

Chapter 19

Never laugh at your significant other's choices because you happen to be one of them.

"What do you mean?" I ask despite knowing exactly what Barney means.

"I gave you something only my brothers know. Hell, I told you things even they don't know about what happened. It's time for you to return the favor."

I gulp and retreat a step. "You want to know something about me no one knows?"

I appreciate him telling me who Ruby is. I do. And, after his story, I'm not worried about him being in love with her any longer. Am I still pissed he called me her name after sex? Kind of. But I think I understand. The man hasn't opened his heart to anyone since she died. There are bound to be some bumps in the road.

Whoa! No bumps in the road. *You don't do relationships, Val. Remember?* True. I don't. Although I'm finding it harder and harder to remember why.

Barney tucks a strand of hair behind my ear. "I want to know everything about you." I gulp. Everything? "But for now, I'll settle for the reason why someone thought it was a good idea to destroy your apartment and all your belongings in it."

"I'm not hiding some big secret from you."

He cocks an eyebrow. "I'm not going to stand by like we did with Phoebe or Chrissie."

"Chrissie has a secret? What is it?"

I'm not an idiot. I know Chrissie has a secret. We all know she does. But none of the women seem to know

A Valentine for Valerie

what it is. I suspect Faith knows as Max tells her everything, but my best friend can keep a secret with the best of them. I'm still hurt she didn't tell me about the gang problems in Saint Louis.

"Chrissie's secrets are hers to tell or not to tell."

Damn. The brothers are loyal to the core. If Chrissie doesn't want anyone to know her secret, her brand-new husband, Wally, will do everything in his power to ensure it stays unknown. And the man has a whole lot of power. I'm not sure how or what, but the man exudes power.

When Barney merely stands there staring at me, I repeat myself, "I'm not hiding any big secret from you."

"But you do have an idea why your apartment was ransacked."

I glance away. He doesn't let me get away with it. He pinches my chin until I'm forced to meet his gaze.

"You can tell me what's going on."

I wrinkle my nose as I study him. "And you won't tell your brothers?"

"I promise I won't tell my brothers unless your safety is compromised."

I purse my lips. "Way to give yourself an out."

He shrugs. "I'm not going to apologize for keeping my woman safe."

"Your woman?" I rear back. "When did I become your woman? Each and every time we get close, you run the other way."

"And where am I right now?" His hands cradle my face. "I'm right here." His lips descend to give me the briefest of kisses. I don't respond. I'm in shock from the whole 'your woman'-thing.

When he lifts his head, he gives me a dazzling smile. His eyes light up with it and it transforms his face from the goofy expression he usually sports to a handsome man I want to spend the rest of my life with.

Whoa, Val! Slow your roll. You don't do

relationships. Geez. How many times am I going to have to remind myself of my no relationship rule with this man around? I shouldn't need a reminder at all.

I clear my throat and step back until Barney has no choice but to drop his hands.

"I reserve the right to discuss the 'I'm your woman, hear me roar'-thing at a later time. Maybe when I'm not standing here in your t-shirt."

He smirks. "I like you in my t-shirt."

He would. It's the human male version of a dog peeing on his territory. "Whatever. Are we done? I need to get changed and get over to my apartment. It's going to take me days to clean up."

"We're not close to being done. One, you are not going to your apartment. Two, the clean-up is already being dealt with. And three, you're not going anywhere until you tell me why you think someone was in your apartment."

"Dude, we've discussed this. No one tells me what to do."

He prowls toward me and backs me into the wall – again. "I will not order you around."

"Oh, really? Was it not you ordering me around less than ten seconds ago? Unless you happen to have an identical twin brother who can transport in and out of here at will."

"I wasn't finished."

"By all means, then finish," I snap at him.

He grins and my eyes narrow. What does he find amusing right now? "You're cute when you're mad. Like a little kitten baring her non-existent claws."

I throw my hands in the air. "For goodness sakes! Can we finish this freaking conversation?"

He shrugs. "Of course. Tell me what I want to know, and we can move on." I huff, and he taps my nose. "Don't forget. We need to meet Aiden down at the station this morning."

The silence stretches between us. Knowing Barney, he'll stand here all day. I'm not about to stand around in his t-shirt all day. I don't care how good it smells.

"I don't know if this is anything," I finally admit.

"Walk me through it."

I give in. "I overheard a client admit he's planning to commit a murder."

Every single muscle in Barney's body locks. "And you didn't think to mention this sooner?"

"I hate to admit this since I know how much you hate defense attorneys, but this isn't the first time I've heard a client say they're going to kill someone."

A muscle in his jaw twitches. "What about this occasion is different?"

"Mr. Davenport—"

"Your boss."

Of course, he remembers who my boss is. The man doesn't forget a thing.

"Yes, my boss. When Sturgess said he was going to kill someone, my boss didn't respond in the way I thought he would."

"Did you say Sturgess? What's his first name?"

"Joseph."

"Tall guy with a crooked nose and a scar across his cheek?"

I nod and Barney swears. And he swears and swears. When he finally pauses, I butt in, "Holy cow. I thought sailors were the ones who could swear but you could give a sailor a run for his money."

"I'm a soldier, not a sailor," he grumbles.

I whip out a salute. "Yes, sir. Whatever you say, sir."

He chuckles. "And I wasn't an officer. You don't call me sir."

I waggle my eyebrows. "What about when we're in bed?"

121

"There's my trouble," he murmurs before kissing my forehead. "Now, back to the story."

Dang. My attempts at distracting him are a big fat failure. I'm usually an ace at distracting a man. But not this man. He's dangerous. And I don't mean dangerous as in he can kill a man with his bare hands, although I'd bet some decent money he can. No, I mean dangerous as in I have to keep reminding myself why I don't do relationships when he's around. Dan. Ger. Ous.

"Fine," I huff. "Mr. Davenport didn't shut Sturgess down when he said he was going to have to kill someone. Sturgess said he needed advice on how not to get caught and Davenport responded – and I quote here – Of course. What were you thinking?"

"Davenport is dirty," Barney grumbles.

"Yeah, I kind of figured that out for myself when I confronted him the next day."

"You confronted him?" he grits out. "Are you out of your mind?"

"Hey! Don't patronize me. I'm not some patsy. I figured Mr. Davenport shut Sturgess down as soon as I left. Because I got my ass out of there the second I could."

He growls. "And what did Davenport say when you talked to him?"

"He told me I was mistaken. I didn't hear what I thought I heard. And, in any event, I need to keep my mouth shut."

"He told you to keep your mouth shut?"

I shrug. "In so many words. He reminded me of the confidentiality clause in my contract."

"Get dressed. We're going to the police station and you're going to tell Aiden everything you told me."

I feel the blood drain from my face. "I can't. Didn't you hear what I just said? If I tell the police, I'm violating my contract. I'll get fired."

"I don't give a crap if you get fired."

I ball my hands into fists. "Well, I do," I growl. "I've

worked really hard to prove myself to Davenport. If I get fired now, I won't find another job in the city. And I'll never be able to afford a house."

"Aiden's a good guy. He'll keep his investigation off the books."

"How can you be certain?"

"This isn't the first time we've used Aiden to help one of the women."

I roll my eyes. "Can you be more mysterious?"

"Tell you what. I'll make you a deal. You talk to Aiden and I'll tell you all about the adventures we've had with Hailey, Phoebe, and Faith."

"You left out Chrissie."

"Nice try." He winks. "You know I can't tell you Chrissie's story."

"Fine. I'll talk to Aiden, but if I end up losing my job, I'm holding you responsible."

"I accept responsibility."

I hold out my hand, and he shakes it. I'm probably making a deal with the devil, but what choice do I have? Barney's right. Someone targeted me. I will not stand by and do nothing. I don't care if I'm the idiot woman in the horror movie opening the basement door when there's a killer on the loose. I'm going down those stairs.

Chapter 20

If I could rearrange the alphabet, I would put U and I together.

Aiden is waiting for us in the lobby of the police station when we arrive. He kisses my cheek in greeting before motioning to the door. "Come on back."

I wave to Barney, but he follows me. "What are you doing?"

"Coming with you."

"I'm a big girl. I can talk to the scary police officer by myself."

He bends close to whisper, "Until we know who ransacked your apartment, I'm not leaving you alone."

Not leaving me alone? Who does he think I am? A toddler who doesn't know how to walk yet? I open my mouth to tell him exactly what I think about his proclamation, but then I notice the noise of the station has calmed down and all eyes are trained on us.

I huff. "We will talk about this 'not leaving me alone' shit at a later time."

He smirks. "I can't wait."

I'm starting to think he gets off on annoying me. "Whatever."

Aiden leads us into a bare-bones room. I survey the room and notice a mirror covering one wall and a table bolted to the ground. I gasp. "Is this an interrogation room?" I approach the mirror and tap on it. "Is this a two-way mirror?" I wave at it. "Is someone observing us right now?"

Barney chuckles before grasping my elbow and

guiding me to a chair. I notice there's a hook in the middle of the table. "What is this for?" Aiden shakes his head at me. And then it hits me. "Is this for a suspect's handcuffs?" I hold out my hands, palms up. "Shackle me, officer. I've been a bad girl." I drop my voice an octave, "a very bad girl."

"We can explore using handcuffs when we're at home, Trouble," Barney whispers into my ear and goosebumps explode on my skin. I've never been into being tied up, but if he talks to me in his deep voice while I'm constrained, I'll definitely consider it.

"Do you want me to leave?" Aiden asks and breaks the moment.

"Can I leave with you?"

Barney glares at me. "No one's leaving until you tell Aiden what you told me this morning."

The amusement flees from Aiden's face. "Do you have an idea about who broke into your apartment?" He barks out the question and suddenly I don't find this room amusing anymore.

I sigh. "Maybe, but you can't tell your wife about it. She'll gossip to the entire group, and I'll lose my job."

Aiden nods. "Whatever happens here remains between us."

"Promise?"

"Unless and until the DA prosecutes whoever did this, the information is confidential."

"Okay," I say and proceed to tell him about the events I told Barney earlier today.

"Well?" Barney prompts when Aiden remains quiet after I finish my story. "Can you pick Sturgess up with this information?"

"I hate to say this but no."

"What do you mean no?" Barney explodes. "He's obviously planning to kill someone, and he broke into Val's apartment."

Aiden holds up his hand. "We have no proof he

125

broke into Val's apartment."

"Maybe he left his fingerprints behind. Can't you use one of those fancy blue light things to find out?" I suggest.

Aiden smiles at me. "The blue light is for finding blood splatter stains."

I gulp. "Blood splatter?"

"Aiden," Barney grumbles.

"Sorry, Val." Aiden clears his throat. "Listen, I appreciate you bringing me information on Sturgess."

"Hold on," I stop him there. "Why do I get the feeling you know exactly who Sturgess is?"

Aiden glances at Barney and I snap my fingers in his face. "Don't look at Barney. He doesn't decide what information I can have or not have. I'm an adult. If I ask you a question, you answer to me. Not to him."

"Sorry, Val," Aiden says but doesn't continue.

"Are you going to tell me who this Sturgess is? Or do I have to ask Chrissie?"

"I thought you didn't want anyone else knowing what's going on?" Barney asks.

I snort. "Chrissie can keep a secret," I tell him before addressing Aiden. "Well?

He clears his throat before admitting, "Sturgess is a known criminal."

I roll my eyes. "Duh. What else?"

"He's the head of a crime syndicate."

I lean forward. "As in the mob?"

"Not exactly."

"I thought mob bosses had their own lawyers. What are they called?" I search my memory for the word. "Got it! Consigliere."

Barney chuckles. "Someone's been watching too many mob movies."

I shrug. "What can I say? The Godfather is one of

the best movie series ever filmed."

His eyes widen. "You watch mob movies?"

"Yeah. And a young Al Pacino and Robert De Niro ain't bad either." I waggle my eyebrows.

"You're a nut."

"It's Ms. Nut to you."

Aiden clears his throat. "Can we get back to the matter at hand, please? My wife's going to get suspicious if I'm gone too long this morning."

Barney crosses his arms over his chest and considers Aiden. "You said you can't pick Sturgess up for breaking into Val's apartment, but what about the attempted murder?"

"There is no attempted murder." Barney growls and Aiden holds up his hand. "In order to prosecute someone for attempted murder, there has to be an intent plus the commission of acts toward the crime. We clearly have the intent, but there were no acts committed."

"As far as you know," I mutter.

"Yes," Aiden agrees. "As far as we know."

I stand. "This was a waste of time. Back to our regularly scheduled program. Aka cleaning my mess of an apartment."

"I already told you your apartment is handled."

"What did you do, Barney? Snap your fingers and poof! The mess disappeared?"

He palms my neck and rests his forehead against mine. "Honey, your apartment and everything in it is a total loss. My brothers are emptying everything out today."

I rear back. "What?" I screech. "What about my clothes? Some of the stuff must be salvageable."

"I asked them to box up your clothing. You can have a look and figure out if there's anything worth saving."

Damnit. It's a good answer, but I'm not going to tell him that. "Whatever."

I stomp toward the door, but Barney grasps my hand to stop me. "We're not done here."

I wrinkle my brow. "Um, yes, we are. Aiden said there's nothing he can do. Which means it's time to hit the mall. I have to work on Monday, and I can hardly go to the office in these clothes." I sweep my hand over my jeans and sweater.

"You aren't going to work on Monday."

I place my palm on Barney's forehead. "Are you okay? Are you sick? Did you hit your head? Because I know you didn't order me to not go to work on Monday."

He captures my hand and places it over his heart. "You know as well as I do your boss is dirty. Until we figure out who broke into your apartment, and why, you need to stay away from him."

"Not happening. I'm not losing my job because of this. For all we know, the break-in was a coincidence and has nothing to do with my job."

He cocks an eyebrow. "You heard a known criminal admit he's going to commit murder in front of your boss and confronted your boss about it and then your apartment was ransacked and it's a coincidence?"

Ugh! When he puts it that way, it does sound pretty damning. It doesn't matter, though. I am not losing my job. Will I be updating my resume and applying to other jobs asap? Yes, yes, I will. But I'm not going to get fired from another job. The groveling I had to do to get hired by Mr. Davenport was embarrassing enough. It won't be happening again.

"Maybe the events are related," I begin and Barney grins. "But I will be going into work." I turn to Aiden. "Don't you think it would be suspicious if I called in sick now? Davenport is distrustful of me as it is."

Aiden grimaces. "You have a point."

"Fine," Barney grumbles. "You can go to work, but—"

"I'm going to stop you there because it sounded

like you're giving me permission to go to my job. I'm sure it's not what you meant."

Barney stares up to the ceiling as if he's praying for patience. I have this effect on men more often. Ask me if I care.

"Okay, but I will accompany you and stay with you while you're at work."

"Stay with me at work? I'm not in danger at work. Besides, how is this going to operate? I can't exactly disguise you as my child who I can't leave alone at home."

"Don't worry. No one will notice me."

"It's not a bad idea," Aiden says.

Great. They're teaming up on me now. It's a fight I can't win. At least, not right now. I'll revisit the issue later.

"Fine. Whatever. We need to leave. I have to buy an entire replacement wardrobe and the mall's already been open for two hours."

Aiden smirks. "Have fun at the mall."

Oh, I will. Shopping is one of my favorite things in the world and judging by the paleness of Barney's face, it's one of his least favorite. Game on, Barney Lewis. Game on.

Chapter 21

You're like a dictionary... you add meaning to my life.

Barney

"Where's *your* woman?" Lenny asks when I sit down at our table at McGraw's that evening.

I ignore his emphasis on my woman. Val is my woman, and I'm not ashamed of it. No, I'm proud to have her by my side. She's still fighting being mine, but I don't mind. I've been alone for thirty years, I can give her some time to adjust. Not a whole lot of time but some.

"At home. She's sorting through a ton of new clothes."

And I do mean a ton. She tried to buy a few outfits, but I insisted she buy more. She said she didn't have the money to buy more. Silly woman. As if I would let her pay for her own clothes after what happened. She made me promise to let her pay her back. She's delusional if she thinks she's paying me back.

"You left her alone?" Lenny sounds incredulous.

Understandable. I would never leave Val alone when danger is lurking. Although, they don't know the whole story. They only know about the break-in last night. I didn't hesitate to tell them since someone had to clean up Val's apartment. I sure as hell wasn't letting her sort through the mess. Not after I found her on the floor of her closet doing her best not to have a breakdown.

"Of course not. Chrissie is there."

Wally chuckles. "Chrissie and clothes? She nearly lost her lunch when Val called to ask for her help."

I shrug. "I wasn't leaving Val alone, but she obviously had enough of me today. It was either Chrissie or Faith. And she doesn't want her best friend knowing what happened."

She's worried she's going to lose her job for telling Aiden what she overheard. And since Faith works at the same law firm, her best friend wasn't an option.

"Faith's worried," Max says as he sets beers down in front of us.

"I know you tell your woman everything, but you can't tell her this. Valerie will have my ass in a sling."

"You catching feelings there, brother?" Lenny asks.

"Like you don't know I caught feelings the moment she sat down next to me at Thanksgiving."

My brothers can read me easier than a book. It's the way it is when you're part of a team. Being able to read a look can save lives. Hell, it did save lives. On multiple occasions. The only reason the five of us are sitting here, safe and sound, is because of the trust we have for each other.

"Considering how fast you were running in the other direction when Val was chasing you, I figured you were too scared to act on your feelings," Lenny says, and my brothers laugh.

It's true. I did run each and every time Val came after me. The feelings I have for her scared the living daylights out of me. I couldn't keep my hands off of her, though. I ended up hurting her by playing hot and cold with her feelings.

There will be no more running, though. The second Val called me last night and I heard how scared she was, my running became a thing of the past. I failed one woman, I will not fail another.

"From what I hear, he didn't have any problems acting on his feelings," Max says and waggles his eyebrows.

I shove his shoulder. "Cut it out. Val isn't some floozy."

Lenny sighs. "He caught feelings all right."

"You jealous?"

"Damn straight, I'm jealous." Lenny never was afraid to let it all hang out. It takes a strong man to admit he's bisexual to his Army brothers, but he didn't hesitate to tell us.

"What about Lexi?"

He frowns. "She can't deal with the real me." In other words, she can't handle his bisexuality.

"Then, she isn't worth your time, brother."

"Amen," Wally agrees. "Now, back to Valerie's issue. How we handling it?"

This is the part where I tell them everything. Val is going to be pissed at me. "There's more to the story."

"There always is," Wally says, and everyone nods in agreement.

"The name Joseph Sturgess mean anything to you?"

It's a rhetorical question. They know exactly who Joseph Sturgess is. We may not be on active duty any longer, but we still keep track of any danger around us and our family. And there's no doubt Sturgess is danger.

"Sturgess is a client of Val's boss, Mr. Davenport," I begin and tell them about what Val overheard.

"You couldn't have told me this before I sent my woman over to your house?" Wally growls before removing his phone from his back pocket.

"Don't growl at me. You knew I wanted Chrissie there to protect Val."

"I don't want my woman going in blind, though." He types a message and hits send. "There. Now she has his description."

"Is this why Val doesn't want anyone knowing? Because it involves her job?" Max asks.

A Valentine for Valerie

"Yeah, she's worried about getting fired. She needs the money because she wants to buy a house."

Sid snorts. "Like you couldn't buy her a house."

It's true. I have plenty of money saved up. After I retired from the military, I had no interest in finding a 'normal' job. Having to wear a suit and sit in an office holds no appeal to me. In fact, it sounds worse than torture. I started playing the stock market instead and discovered I'm good at it.

"I can't exactly buy her a house for our first date." I would, but Val would run screaming the other way.

Sid chuckles. "Why not? Your ass is already in a sling for telling us what's happening."

"I warned her. If she's in trouble, I'm bringing in my brothers."

"She's still going to be pissed," he pushes.

"Don't care. She needs to be safe."

"Faith is going to be happy," Max says.

I cock an eyebrow at him. Faith is going to be happy her best friend's in danger?

"Not about Val being in danger. She'll be happy Val finally found love and is going to stay in Milwaukee. She missed her best friend."

Found love? I wait for the panic, but it doesn't come. I knew I was falling before, but the lack of panic confirms it.

"If you women are done talking about your feelings, can we discuss how we're going to handle Sturgess now?"

Wally's full of shit. He had no problems deep diving into his feelings when he met Chrissie. He also didn't waste any time putting a ring on it. I don't know how he got away with surprising Chrissie with a wedding, but I know better than to pull the same stunt on Val. I don't know why she's afraid of relationships, but she is.

"We don't have the manpower to tackle Sturgess." As much as I'd enjoy handling the man, he's in charge of a criminal organization. If we go after him, a shit ton of trouble will rain down upon us.

"I can get the manpower," Wally claims.

Unlike the rest of us, Wally never really 'retired'. He continued to be involved in black ops. Chrissie put an end to his work, though.

"I thought you retired."

Sid makes the sound of a whip. "Someone's whipped."

Everyone ignores him since Sid hasn't been without a wife or girlfriend for more than a week at a time.

"I can make some calls," Wally offers.

"Not yet. We don't know what Sturgess thinks Val heard. The break-in at her apartment may be the end of it. Until we know for certain, Val will have herself a tail twenty-four seven."

Sid rubs his hands together. "She's going to lose her mind. This is going to be fun. Can you put up some cameras when you tell her?"

I don't deign to respond to his craziness.

"Is everyone up for helping out?"

Lenny frowns. "Do you really need to ask?"

I don't but asking is the polite thing to do. I gaze around the table and watch as each man lifts his chin in my direction. Relief fills me. With my brothers at my back, I won't fail another woman.

"Good. It's settled. Now, has anyone heard the joke about the spy who …"

There are groans all around, and I grin. Telling corny inappropriate jokes is the best way to get my brothers annoyed and annoying them is how I show I care.

Chapter 22

I know this is going to sound cheesy, but I think you're the gratest.

I wake up on Sunday in the exact same position as Saturday morning – cuddled into Barney. But this time instead of trying to sneak out of the bed, I settle in. I know this thing with him isn't going to last long. I might as well enjoy it while I can.

"Good morning, Trouble," Barney whispers in my ear before biting on the lobe.

I groan and grind my ass into his hardness, but he withdraws. I mewl. "Where are you going?"

"We're taking things slow."

"We've already had sex," I remind him. I vote for a repeat. The first time was pretty dang spectacular. Although Barney doesn't need to hear those thoughts.

"But now we're involved."

"Involved? You're scared of me, remember?" And yes, I realize I'm being a hypocrite here. I'm not scared of Barney, but I sure as shit am afraid of a relationship. I have my reasons. And they're good, too.

"Not anymore."

I bury my face in my pillow and scream. I may flail my arms and legs about a bit, too. Barney slaps my ass and I squeal.

"Come on, sleepy pie. Get dressed and we'll go out to breakfast."

Breakfast? Nope. Breakfast spells relationship. "No need. I can dash down to the bakery on the corner and grab us some fresh bagels."

"Okay. Let me get dressed."

I stand from the bed. "Dude, I can go to a bakery by myself."

"I told you, until this matter with Sturgess is settled, I'll be tailing you. In fact," he clears his throat, "either me or one of my brothers will be with you at all times."

I narrow my eyes on him. "One of your brothers? Please tell me you didn't tell everyone my business."

"Not everyone," he hedges.

I hit him with a pillow. "You promised you wouldn't tell anyone."

He grabs the pillow and uses his hold on it to draw me near. "No, honey. I promised I wouldn't tell anyone as long as you're not in danger. Aiden admitted yesterday he can't arrest Sturgess based on the information you provided, which means you're in danger."

"How long is this going to last?"

"Until I know you're safe."

"Which will be forever. I researched Sturgess while you were gone yesterday. The guy has been accused of all sorts of nasty crimes, but he's never been convicted of a single one. I'd be surprised if the guy has ever gotten a speeding ticket."

"Hopefully, Friday's break-in was a warning, and when the police don't show up at Sturgess' door, he'll assume you didn't tell anyone what you heard, and this will all blow over."

I can tell he doesn't believe his own words. Shit. So much for Milwaukee being my clean slate.

"Fine. Who's going furniture shopping with me today?"

"You're not going furniture shopping."

"Dude, yes, I am. I can't live in my apartment with no furniture and you told me your brothers emptied my place out yesterday except for boxes of my shredded clothes."

A Valentine for Valerie

My poor clothes. Sniff. Sniff. I'm going to need years to rebuild my wardrobe.

Barney palms my neck. "You are not returning to your apartment. I told you. You're staying here until this matter is settled."

Bad idea. I can barely resist the guy as it is. If I spend time living in his space, I'm going to get attached, and attached is bad. It's very, very bad.

"If I can't go home, I'll stay with Faith. She's got plenty of room in their apartment."

He crosses his arms over his chest. "And listen to Faith and Max enjoy their engagement every night?"

I shrug. "Doesn't bother me."

He growls. "You won't be listening to another man have sex while we're involved."

Sigh. Not this again. "We're not involved."

His bizarre response? "And you're not buying any furniture."

Ugh! Here we go again. Barney wouldn't let me buy any of the clothes I picked out yesterday either. I tried to buy a few outfits to tide me over until my next paycheck, but Mr. My Way Or The Highway said he was paying, and I needed more clothes. I refused and he started yanking clothes off the racks willy-nilly. It was scary. He didn't check the sizes or colors or shapes at all!

We finally compromised. I let him pay for my new clothes, but I kept all the receipts and will be paying him back. Based on how many things he made me buy, I'm going to be in debt to him forever. Which was probably his plan in the first place. Sneaky man.

"I will buy my own furniture. The big stores have layaway programs. It'll be fine."

"We'll talk about this later. Let me get showered and dressed and then I'll take you out to breakfast."

He doesn't give me a chance to respond before he saunters to the bathroom and shuts the door behind him. He didn't even offer me the opportunity to shower with him.

What kind of relationship is this?

I need a coffee. I cannot deal with Barney without caffeine. Once I'm caffeinated, I'll be able to talk circles around him.

I groan when I find his coffeemaker. It's one of those old-fashioned drip machines. I search through his drawers until I find the coffee and filters. Who has a filter coffee machine anymore? Once the coffee is brewing, it's time to explore his place.

I didn't bother snooping around yesterday. Silly me. I thought I wouldn't be spending any more time here. There isn't much to investigate. The studio space is big, but it's pretty empty. There's a kitchen with a bar with two stools in front of it. A large sofa. And a bed.

There aren't any pictures on the wall, and there are no knick-knacks anywhere to be found. His bedside tables are empty. The coffee table has one book on it – some military biography – and nothing else. This place has zero personality.

But wait. There's a computer in the corner. It's one of those set-ups you see on television for a hacker with three computer monitors.

I hear the bathroom door open and whirl around to watch Barney stroll out of the room. He's only dressed in a pair of jeans hanging low on his hips. His abs bunch as he walks to the dresser to find a top to wear.

"You like what you see?" he asks with his back to me.

Damn right, I do. His back is as muscled as his front. I never knew back muscles could be sexy. I've been missing out. He puts on a sweater and his muscles disappear. I sigh and he chuckles.

"I can strut around topless for you later."

Good idea. And without shoes and socks, too. I do love a man with bare feet.

He saunters over to me and kisses my forehead. "Bathroom's free. Go on in and I'll bring your coffee when it's ready."

At the mention of coffee, my brain finally switches from its sexy visions of Barney to more pressing matters.

"How is it you have the oldest coffee machine in the world, but you have this computer set-up?" I motion to his desk. "Are you a hacker or something?"

His eyes sparkle. "Or something."

I roll my eyes. "Are you going to be all secretive? You're not a super-secret soldier like Wally are you?"

"Nah. I do day trading."

My brow wrinkles. "Day trading as in the stock market?"

"You didn't think I spent all my time playing poker with my brothers, did you?"

Actually, I did. "You do seem to be at McGraw's every time I show up there."

"What else am I going to do? Hang around here all day?"

"I did notice your place is pretty barren. I didn't figure you for a minimalist."

He shrugs. "I'm not. I've just never ..." He pauses.

"It's okay. You don't need to explain." I start toward the bathroom, but he stops me with a hand on my shoulder.

"I never wanted a home again, not after Ruby."

I swallow. It always comes back to Ruby, doesn't it? I'll always live in her shadow. *Live in her shadow?* What am I thinking? I will not be living in her shadow because I'm not in a relationship with Barney no matter what he thinks.

Barney squeezes my shoulder. "Stop whatever it is you're thinking."

I narrow my eyes. "How do you know what I'm thinking?"

"You're easy to read, Trouble."

"Whatever. I'm going for my shower." I walk off

before he can stop me.

"I'm not living in the past," he shouts at me. Fine. My interest is piqued. I stop and glance over my shoulder. "I know you think I'm constantly comparing you to Ruby, but I'm not."

"I'm not..." I cut myself off. It is what I'm thinking, but I need to shut up before he thinks I'm agreeing to this relationship because I'm not.

"When I'm with you, the only person I think about is you."

"Okay." Maybe if I agree, he'll stop speaking.

"I know you don't believe me now, but I'll convince you."

"Yeah. Yeah. Whatever."

I hurry into the bathroom and slam the door behind me because I'm terrified he's going to do exactly as he says. Convince me I'm his. Time for a good long shower during which I can spend my time building my walls and reminding myself why relationships are bad.

Chapter 23

Are you from Starbucks? Because I like you a latte.

Barney drives to a strip mall with a diner for breakfast.

"Dude, we didn't need to drive somewhere for breakfast. We could have grabbed a bite to eat at a place near your apartment."

When he parks and I reach for the door handle, he stops me. "Wait there."

His grumpy order has my stomach warming and tingles exploding down my body until they reach my center. Before I have a chance to calm myself down, he opens my door. He squeezes my waist to lift me out of the car.

"I can get out of a truck by myself," I bitch to hide how my skin is tingling at his close proximity.

He smirks before grabbing my hand and leading me into the diner. We settle into a booth near the window.

The waitress arrives with coffee and menus. "What can I get you two lovebirds?"

Lovebirds? Is she talking about us? I survey the room, but there's no one else near us. Shit. She is talking about us.

"Coffee for now. We need a minute with the menus," Barney answers. She pours the coffees and leaves.

I keep my eyes trained on my menu. *Deep breaths, Val.* A waitress saying you and Barney are lovebirds doesn't make us lovebirds. I hear Barney laugh, and I look up from my menu. When I see the amusement on his face, I slap the menu on the table and glare at him.

"What could possibly be funny right now?"

"You. You're totally panicking for nothing."

"I'm not panicking." My racing heart calls me a liar. "I'm hungry. What's good here?"

Lucky for him, he doesn't call me out on my obvious lie.

Thirty minutes later, I've eaten my weight in pancakes and syrup. I'm stress eating, but I'm not going to beat myself up about it. My apartment and everything in it was destroyed. And this infuriating but incredibly sexy man sitting across from me wants to have a relationship with me. I deserve a little stress eating.

"You're going to have to roll me into your truck," I tell Barney as he helps me to my feet.

"We have a few stops first," he says as we exit the diner and he turns to the right.

"The truck is over there." I point to it. "Are you going senile, old man? Did you forget where you parked it?"

He halts and drops my hand to palm my neck. "I can show you how I'm most definitely not an old man in front of everyone at this mall."

I retreat. "No, thanks. I'm good."

He chuckles as he captures my hand again and continues in the opposite direction of his truck. He opens the door to the next store.

"What are we doing in a fabric store?" I ask as I survey the place. This is my kind of store. Since I can't afford to be the fashionista I want to be on my salary, I've learned to be creative with fabric.

"You'll see," he says as he walks toward the service counter.

I hang back until I notice the employee hand Barney a large box. My eyes widen when I realize what's in the box. "What are you doing?"

I try to steal the box away from him, but he holds it above his head like it weighs nothing. I know from experience it does not weigh nothing.

"There's no way you can fix the clothes the burglar ruined without a sewing machine and your sewing machine is currently at the bottom of the city dump."

"You can't buy me a new sewing machine," I hiss at him.

"I'm not buying it for you."

Phew. "Okay. Good then. Let's go."

"It's my Christmas present to you."

I glare at him and count to five. Counting to five doesn't calm me down one little bit. This man is infuriating. "Christmas has come and gone."

"And I'm correcting my mistake of not buying you a Christmas present right now."

"A sewing machine is too expensive for a gift."

"I choose how much money I spend on my woman for her gifts."

I throw my hands in the air. "I'm not your woman." When will he get it through his thick skull?

"You will be." He winks before marching away. By the time I catch up to him, he's already checking out.

He tags my hand and hums as we exit the store with him carrying the box for the sewing machine.

"I am not happy," I complain as we drive away from the strip mall.

He squeezes my thigh. "I will work my ass off to ensure you're happy for the rest of your life."

I cross my arms over my chest. "Not what I meant, and you know it." And the butterflies in my stomach are not doing a happy dance at the idea of this man doing his best to make me happy for the rest of my life.

He shrugs and takes the next exit.

"Where are we going now? This isn't the way to your apartment."

"One more errand. Then, we can go home and relax for the rest of Sunday."

We can relax? *Home?* Barney is delusional. *We* aren't a we. And his place isn't my home.

"We're going grocery shopping?" I ask as he parks.

He doesn't bother answering my stupid question. And it is a stupid question. We're parked in front of a grocery store after all. He comes around the front of the vehicle and frowns when he notices me standing there.

"Next time wait for me to open your door." He nabs my hand and leads me to the entrance.

It's oddly intimate walking into a grocery store holding hands. I've never been grocery shopping with a man before. Grocery shopping spells relationship with a capital R. Why else would you buy things like toilet paper together unless you're serious about each other?

My heart constricts and breathing becomes difficult, but I power through it. The store is packed. I don't want to have a conversation about our situation in front of all these strangers. And, make no mistake about it, Barney wouldn't hesitate to have the conversation here. I'm supposed to be the fearless one. Not him.

Barney doesn't notice my hesitation or, if he does, he ignores it. He grabs a cart and steers it toward the entrance.

"Any special requests for breakfast tomorrow?" he asks.

I stare at him with my mouth gaping open.

"Any requests for dinner tonight?"

My throat does not work. Is he seriously asking me these questions in front of everyone?

"I'll keep asking until you answer."

"Fine," I huff and steal the cart from him before marching into the store.

By the time we're in line to check-out fifteen minutes later, I'm gasping for breath. I raced up and down the aisles as fast as I could. Every time Barney asked me a question about what brand I preferred, my feet sped up. Grocery shopping is entirely too intimate for me. Sweat is literally breaking out on my brow. It's not because of how quick I went through this store either.

When we return home— *No, not home, Val.* It's a temporary residence.

When we return to Barney's apartment, it's to find boxes piled up against the hallway outside his door.

"What's this?" I ask. I'm almost afraid of his answer, but this woman is not a chicken. I face my problems head-on.

"Your clothes."

I squeal. "My clothes!"

"Let me put the groceries away and then I'll carry in the boxes for you," Barney says as he unlocks his door.

I ignore him and carry the first box inside. I place it on the table before opening it. The clothes haven't been folded. Everything has been stuffed willy-nilly into the box. I dump the contents on the table and begin sorting through it. I hold up a skirt. It's been torn, but the tear is along the seam. I can totally fix this.

I sort the clothes into two piles – those worth saving, and those even I can't save. By the time I've finished with this box, Barney has brought in the rest of the boxes and stacked them next to the table.

"Where do you want this?" he asks as he holds up the sewing machine.

I want to tell him to return the machine to the store, but when I look down at the pile of clothes needing some tender loving care, I can't. I point to a corner of the table.

Barney touches my shoulder sometime later. I don't startle. This delicate piece of fabric will be ruined if I do.

"You need a break. Time for lunch."

I sigh as I study the pile of clothes. I don't need a break. I need two more arms and another sewing machine.

Barney doesn't let me argue. He switches off the machine and helps me to my feet. "I made us tuna melts and fries."

He leads me to the sofa where he's set out our food and some sodas on the coffee table. "The game or a movie?" he asks as he picks up the remote control.

The game? Does he think I have the first clue about what game he's talking about? I don't. Silly man. He should never give me a choice. I will never choose a sporting event.

"Movie." And because I'm more than annoyed with him trying to railroad my life, I add, "A romantic comedy."

He hands me the remote. "You pick the movie. I don't have a fucking clue what a romantic comedy is."

I giggle. This is going to be fun.

Chapter 24

My feet are getting cold...because you knocked my socks off.

Barney kisses my shoulder and I grumble, "five more minutes."

I'm not ready to get up. It's still dark outside, and I didn't sleep well last night. It's hard to get a good night's rest when you have to work with a boss who's probably in cahoots with criminals the next day.

Duh. Of course, my boss works with criminals. He's a defense attorney after all. But I didn't realize he worked with dangerous criminals. The type of guys who kill people because they get in the way of his criminal empire.

And – this is a biggie – I thought Mr. Davenport helped his clients to navigate the legalities of the criminal justice system. Because this is what defense attorneys are for. Helping people who have been accused of a crime. It's a vital part of the criminal justice system. They're not supposed to help criminals with the actual commission of a crime.

"How much time do you need to get ready?" Barney's voice is scratchy with sleep. It makes my skin tingle. Maybe I don't need five more minutes of sleep. Maybe I need a few minutes of sexy times this morning to wake me up.

"Forty-five minutes," I mutter.

"You've got thirty minutes and then we're leaving."

What? Thirty minutes? I can't get ready in such a short time! My eyes fly open and I jump out of the bed. Or, I try to. My legs get caught in the comforter and I end up sprawled on the floor. I climb to my knees and use the bed to help me stand.

"Thirty minutes! Why didn't you wake me up earlier?"

He smirks at me, and I narrow my eyes on him. "I tried, Trouble. I tried."

"Why didn't my alarm go off?"

"Because I switched it off."

"You did what?" I screech.

He shrugs. "You tossed and turned all night. You finally fell into a deep sleep around 3 a.m. I'm not going to apologize for making sure you get at least a few hours of decent rest before you have to work."

I throw my arms in the air. I can't argue with Barney when he's being all sweet and taking care of me. I need to find an outfit to wear and get dressed. I don't need to be arguing with Barney first thing on a Monday morning.

I rush to my bags in the corner of the room, but there are no bags in the corner of the room. "Where are my clothes?"

"In the dresser." He points to his dresser.

Barney's dresser. When did I put my clothes in his dresser? The answer is easy. I didn't. Where does he get off putting all my clothes away? Fortunately for him, I don't have time to argue with him about this right now. I find a blouse and skirt to wear and grab a bra and panties before slamming the drawers closed and running to the bathroom.

I'm rushing through my shower when I hear the bathroom door open. "Your coffee's on the vanity. Milk and sugar like you drink it."

"Thank you," I force myself to shout.

Why does Barney have to be attentive and sweet? Is he deliberately trying to tempt me into throwing my rule about no relationships away? I'm not in the market for a relationship and I never will be. *Yeah, right, Val.* You keep telling yourself that. Maybe you'll even believe it after a while.

I'm scarfing down a bagel when someone knocks

on the door. "Who's knocking on your door on Monday morning before 8 a.m.?"

Barney saunters to the door. "It's Wally. He's your shadow for the day."

"I thought you were going to be my shadow." And, dang it, why do I sound upset about this change of plans?

Barney pivots and comes to stand in front of me. He places a hand on my cheek. "I'm sorry, honey. I have some work to do today. I promise Wally will keep you safe."

"I'm perfectly safe at work."

He taps my nose. "I know you are because Wally will be with you."

I finish my bagel while he lets Wally in. Wally doesn't come further than the doorway. He stands there with his arms across his chest playing the part of my bodyguard. He better not act like this all day. Mr. Davenport will have no doubt I sold him out.

I stand and throw my purse over my shoulder. "I'm ready."

Before I can step toward the door, Barney stops me with a hand on my arm. "Have a good day, honey."

His lips meet mine in a gentle kiss. "Be good, Trouble," he whispers against my lips.

"Never."

He chuckles before grasping my hand and escorting me to the door. "Take care of her, brother."

Wally dips his chin. "With my life."

I roll my eyes. "I'm going to work. There's no danger."

Wally places his hand on my lower back and leads me toward the elevator. "And I'm here to ensure it stays that way."

He drives me to work and parks in my parking spot in the garage below our building. "This is your spot?" he asks as he switches off the engine.

149

"Um, yeah. I literally gave you directions to it less than a minute ago."

He frowns. "I don't like it."

"Hey! I'm lucky I got a parking spot. They're usually reserved for the lawyers and legal support staff." Since Mr. Davenport was desperate for a secretary to start as soon as possible and I agreed to begin immediately, I was able to negotiate some perks such as this parking spot.

"I meant how far you are from the stairs and elevator. This corner is dark and dangerous."

I hold up my hand to stop his lecture. "It's bad enough I have Barney harping on about my safety, I don't need you to do it, too."

He shakes his head. "Barney has his hands full with you."

"Whatever."

While we ride the elevator to my floor, I explain to him, "You can't be seen being my bodyguard all day. What will my boss think?"

He winks at me. "Don't worry. I won't be seen."

The man is several inches over six feet and isn't skinny by anyone's definition. Unless he's a superhero who can make himself invisible or has an invisibility cloak, he's going to be seen.

The elevator dings open and I step out. I point to the right. "My office is over there."

When he doesn't respond, I glance over my shoulder to find Wally isn't there. Holy cow. Maybe he is a superhero.

I'm not at my desk for five minutes before Faith finds me.

"Hey, Faith. Happy Monday."

"We need to talk."

Great. I knew this was coming. "Is everything okay with the wedding? You're not getting cold feet, are you?

It's understandable considering your first marriage to Silas."

I usually avoid saying the name of her first husband, but desperate times are upon me.

"I do not have cold feet. I can't wait to marry Max."

I smile. "He is the best."

"Better than Barney?" She waggles her eyebrows.

This is why I tried to distract her with the marriage talk. She couldn't have missed how Barney was cozied up to me on Friday night at Hailey's birthday party. No matter how much I shoved him off, there he was.

"We're at work, Faith. It's not the appropriate place to discuss my love life."

"Then, let's talk about why you have a tail."

I sit up and scan the room. Wally promised me no one would spot him. Shit. Did everyone see him? I certainly don't spot him anywhere at the moment. Where is he?

"How do you know?"

"Aha," she shouts.

I shush her. "Did you forget we're at work?" I hiss.

Although most of the attorneys haven't graced us with their presence yet, Mr. Davenport is already in his office. He was in his office when I arrived. I know because I barely set my purse down before he barked at me to get him some coffee.

"What's going on?" she whispers.

"I don't know what you're talking about. I need to get back to work." I focus on my computer, but Faith doesn't leave. Of course, she doesn't. It was all fine and dandy for her to run away from Saint Louis and not tell me her reasons, but lord forbid I keep a secret from her.

She waves her hand in front of my computer. "Don't ignore me. I know something's going on."

"I cannot and will not discuss it with you here."

"Lunch then. We'll go to the sandwich shop and

you can tell me all about why you have a guard on you."

"I don't know if I can do lunch. I'm awful busy."

The intercom on my phone beeps. "Yes, Mr. Davenport?"

"If you're done gossiping, could you get me the file for my next meeting?"

Gossiping? Did Mr. Davenport hear what Faith and I are talking about? Nah. He couldn't have. The door was closed, and it's not like he has a bionic ear.

"File, Ms. Cook," he repeats and brings me out of my thoughts.

I clear my throat. "Right away."

"Lunch," Faith repeats before she saunters off.

Great. I'm going to have to figure out a way to avoid her until this situation is settled. I could tell her what's happening, but I don't want her to worry about me. She's got enough going on in her life with her upcoming wedding and making sure Ollie is adjusting to having Max in his life.

Chapter 25

If I had a star for every time you brightened my day, I'd have a galaxy in my hand.

A hush falls over the office right before six arrives to signal the end of the day. I hear whispers, but I don't stop what I'm doing. I'm trying to finish one last task for Mr. Davenport before I can go home. Wally appeared at five and asked me when I'll be finished with work. I promised him I'd be done by six. And I'm going to keep my promise.

A shadow falls over my desk. "Two more minutes, Wally. I'm nearly finished."

I hear a chuckle. I know this chuckle. I drag my eyes away from my computer to find Barney standing in front of my desk holding a bouquet of red roses. He's also dressed up in navy blue slacks and a gray button-down shirt. Someone cleans up nicely – very nicely.

"What's going on?"

I scan the room and discover the other secretaries are leaning over their desks listening in on our conversation. Several of them give me thumbs-ups.

"I'm here to pick you up for our first date."

"First date? I don't date. I don't do relationships." How many times am I going to have to repeat myself before I believe it? No, not me. Before Barney believes me.

He smirks. "Good. This is going to be fun."

"What do you mean?" I'm terrified I already know the answer.

"Hurry up and finish. I'll arrange these and then

you can put them on your desk where you can see them while you're working all day."

The words are barely out of his mouth before another secretary, Dawn, rushes over. "Let me show you where the kitchen is." Her words are breathy, and her face is flushed.

My eyes narrow as I watch her drooling over my man like he's a juicy steak she can't wait to take a bite out of. Hold up. My man? Barney isn't my man, and I'd be smart to remember it. I can't have a man, remember? Because men turn into monsters.

I force myself to concentrate on completing the memos for Mr. Davenport, so I can finish up for the day. I double check everything before sending the documents to him for review. Since he's not here, I shut down my computer and straighten my desk.

By the time I finish, Barney is sauntering toward me holding a vase with flowers. "Where did you find a vase?" is the idiotic question that comes out of my mouth.

"I bought it. I didn't know if you'd have one here. But now you do." He sets the flowers on the corner of my desk. Why do I get the feeling the flowers are some sort of claiming?

I purse my lips. "I don't need to have a vase at my office."

He smirks. "Okay." He scans my desk. "You ready?"

"Yep." I stand.

Barney picks my coat off the coat stand and holds it open for me before helping me into it. He kisses my neck. "Hi, honey."

Goosebumps break out at the feel of his breath on my skin. "Hi." My voice sounds like I swallowed a frog. I try again, "Hi."

He laces his fingers through mine. "Come on. I have a surprise for you."

"What if I hate surprises?"

"You'll love this one."

Jerk. He knows I love surprises. Who doesn't? The devil. That's who.

We exit the building to discover it's snowing. It's also freezing, but I ignore the cold when I spot the horse-drawn carriage in front of me. My jaw falls open when Barney leads me toward it.

"We're going on a carriage ride?"

He doesn't bother responding to my remark as he helps me into the carriage. He sits next to me before gathering the blankets around us. Once we're settled in, he nods to the coachman who clicks his tongue and we're off.

"It's a bit too cold for champagne," Barney says as he draws a picnic basket near. "But I have peppermint patties."

I have no idea what a peppermint patty is. "Peppermint patties? We're going to drink Charlie Brown's school friend?"

He chuckles. "A peppermint patty is a hot chocolate with peppermint schnapps."

"Sounds yummy."

He hands me a mug and I take a sip. The taste of chocolate and peppermint coats my tongue. "It's good."

"I also brought some snacks to tide us over until dinner."

"I'm good," I say as I snuggle into the blankets with my hot chocolate.

Barney wraps his arm around me and pulls me near. I should probably protest, but I'm too warm and comfortable to lie to him about how wonderful this experience is right now.

We remain quiet as the carriage travels through traffic until we're on Lincoln Memorial Drive. We turn north and follow the lake.

"When we're next to the lake, I can view the stars," I say as I stare up at the sky.

"Do you enjoy gazing at the stars?"

I smile at him. "Not a whole lot of stargazing to be done when you live in the city."

"Have you always lived in a city?"

"Yep. Born and bred in Saint Louis. And then I came here. What about you? Are you from here?"

"I grew up out east in a small town in Maryland, but when I retired, I followed my brothers here. Max and Hailey were already here, and it was a good place for us to land."

"Do you have any family left in Maryland?"

"A few cousins. I visit them once a year in the summer. I'll introduce you when we travel to Maryland this summer."

Whoa. Down boy. This summer? It's currently January. Did he forget I don't do relationships? Certainly nothing long-term.

"Did you forget I don't date?"

He smirks. "What do you call what we're doing right now then?" Shit. He's right. I try to pull away from him, but he tightens his arm. "There's no reason to be afraid. I'll never hurt you. At least not on purpose. I'm a man. I'm bound to make stupid mistakes."

"You mean stupid mistakes as in forcing a date on me?" I snarl.

"Forcing? Look where you are, Trouble." He squeezes my shoulder for emphasis. "Until I mentioned the d-word, you were perfectly content in my arms."

Irritating man. Proving he's right and I'm wrong. Who does he think he is? Being right.

"We're here," he announces.

We're parked in front of a round, brick building. "Where's here? And what are we doing here?"

"You'll see." He lifts the blankets off me and folds them before placing them in the corner. Then, he helps me out of the carriage.

"We'll be back in an hour," he tells the coachman.

"What are we doing?" I ask again, but Barney doesn't answer. He takes my hand and leads me to the entrance.

We enter a building, and I scan the area. "Are we in a school?"

"Kind of."

We walk down the hallway toward a set of double doors. Above the door is a sign *Manfred Olson Planetarium.* Planetarium? As in stargazing?

The door opens and an attendant ushers us in. The place is completely empty.

"What did you do? Rent the place out for the night?" He shrugs, and I slap his shoulder. "You did!"

"This way we can have a picnic under the Northern Lights," he says and motions to a blanket spread out on the floor in the middle of the room. On top of the blanket is an old-fashioned wicker picnic basket.

"Barney Lewis, are you a romantic?"

His cheeks flame, but he keeps his gaze steady on me. "So, sue me. I want to give you romance. Something tells me you haven't gotten a whole lot of romance in your life and you deserve it."

The attendant behind us clears her throat. "If you could take your seats, we can begin."

Barney directs me toward the picnic blanket. He helps me to lower myself to the floor before sitting next to me. He opens the picnic basket and lays out the food. There are chicken wings, potato salad, coleslaw, and a tray of veggies with hummus. My stomach rumbles at the display.

He chuckles before removing a dish. He makes me a plate with a little helping from each dish. After he hands me the food, he digs two wine glasses and a bottle of red out of the basket.

"What else do you have in there?"

I'm joking, but he answers, "some brownies and

chocolate chip cookies."

Before I can answer, the lights dim and the 'sky' above us comes to life with blue and violet colors. My mouth drops open, and I forget all about my dinner. "This is beautiful."

"It's amazing in person."

"You've seen the Northern Lights in person?"

He nods. "I'll take you on a trip to Norway to see them. Tromso, Norway in the heart of the aurora zone in the Norwegian Arctic is one of the best places to view the lights. They're best seen from September through April. Let me know when you can get time off from work and I'll make the arrangements."

He's crazy. There's no other explanation for talking about a trip to Maryland in the summer and a trip to Norway. Norway? I've never been outside the US before, let alone been to Europe.

He chuckles at my inability to speak. He hands me a glass of wine before pouring one for himself. I stop him. "You shouldn't drink and drive."

"No driving for me. Our carriage awaits."

Oh gosh. He's not kidding. There is literally a carriage waiting to drive us home. I open my mouth to complain about how this isn't a date and I didn't agree to it, but I snap my mouth shut before any words can form. I am not complaining to him about this. Not when he went to such great lengths to make our first date special.

Our first date? I don't date. I ignore the reminder. For this one time and one time only, I'm going to enjoy myself and forget about how men become monsters.

Chapter 26

I'm no photographer, but I can picture us together.

"Good morning, honey." Barney's voice sounds entirely too happy. Doesn't he know it's illegal to be happy in the morning until a copious amount of caffeine has been drunk? And even then it's a precarious situation.

I bury my face in my pillow. "I'm not ready to adult yet."

"You're going to want to be awake for this." The lilt in his voice says he's teasing, but he's also using the deep, scratchy morning voice I find way too sexy.

I perk up. Now, I'm interested. After Barney wowed me with an awesome first date, he brought me home, tucked me up in bed, kissed my forehead, and …. There is no and. Because nothing else happened. There were no sexy times.

Barney said he's courting me and there will be no sex again until I admit I'm his. I guess I'm going to the naughty shop to buy a new 'friend' because I will never admit I'm his. Never, I say. I'll have to live off the memories of our sexy times together until I'm old and gray. Oh, who am I kidding? I will never be gray.

I force one eye open. Barney's standing next to the bed smiling down at me. Too bad he's covering up those ab muscles with a t-shirt. I open the other eye.

"What is it? Why do I want to be awake? And what time is it?"

Barney helps me to sit up in bed. He even plumps up a pillow and sticks it behind me. "Wait right there."

"Where do you think I'm going to go?" I shout at

his retreating back.

When he turns around, he's carrying a tray. A breakfast tray to be exact. It's loaded with all kinds of goodies. There's a bagel. A must have since I live on bagels. But there's also pancakes and bacon. Plus, coffee. There must be coffee despite how crappy the coffee from his coffee machine is.

"Here you go, Trouble," he says as he sets the tray on my lap.

"Hold on," I tell him. "I need to have a sip of your crappy coffee before I can deal with you and your shiny personality this morning."

I pick up the coffee mug and sniff. Huh. It doesn't smell like muddy water as it has every other morning I've been staying with Barney. I take a sip and the delicious nectar of the gods fills my mouth.

"Oh my god. This coffee is good. How did you go out for coffee and I didn't hear you leave?"

He smirks as he sits on the bed at my feet. "I didn't go out for coffee."

"You certainly didn't make this coffee with your ancient machine."

"I didn't. I bought a new coffeemaker yesterday."

"About time."

"Now, you'll have good coffee every morning."

I freeze. The piece of bacon I was about to munch down on hanging in the air. "What did you say?" He opens his mouth, but I drop the bacon and glare at him. "No, don't repeat yourself. I don't need to hear it again to know you're cray-cray."

"There's nothing crazy about wanting to make sure my woman has everything she needs."

Damnit. There goes my chance of eating this delicious tray of food while it's still hot. It's fight time.

"I am not your woman. You need to stop with the full court press. It's never going to happen."

"It's going to happen. I've witnessed my brothers Max, Wally, and Sid fall in love over the past year and I want the same thing."

"I thought you were afraid of love."

He grins. "No, honey. It's you who's afraid of love."

He's not wrong. Fudging hell.

He places a hand on my legs and squeezes. "Tell you what. Let's make a deal." I push the tray away and cross my arms over my chest. I am not happy with where this is going. The last time we made a deal, he ended up buying me an entire new wardrobe.

"You tell me why you don't want a relationship with me and, if the reason is good, I'll back off."

I cock an eyebrow at him. "You'll back off?"

"As long as the reason's a good one."

Oh, it is. "Are you positive you want to make this deal?"

"One-hundred percent. I want to know what has you running scared and who I have to kill."

"Why would you have to kill someone?"

"A gorgeous, fun, full of life woman like you who isn't attached in her forties and is afraid of a relationship? Someone hurt you. Someone hurt you bad."

"What if the person who hurt me was my mom?" I throw the question out there, expecting him to back down. He doesn't, though. Of course not. And I thought I was the fearless one.

"Then, I'll make sure she never hurts you again."

I narrow my eyes on him. "Did you seriously just offer to get rid of my mom?"

"Stop stalling."

I sip on my coffee as I consider how to answer. The only person who knows this story is Faith, and I only told her after I decided to drink my weight in Cosmopolitans. Don't judge. Cosmos are yummy and therefore impossible to resist. I've never told a man this story. I never planned to tell a man this story. Most men hear you don't want a relationship and smile before asking you back to their place.

"How much time ya got?"

"As much time as you need, honey. As much as you need."

"To start with, I should probably say I have no idea who my dad is." His eyes widen, and I wave my hands at him. "No, don't feel sorry for me. If you're going to pity me, this isn't going to work."

"I don't pity you," he grumbles. "You're a strong, independent woman. I admire you."

His words hit me in the chest and warmth blossoms. No one's ever said they admired me before. It's a powerful feeling to be admired. I have to take a breath before I launch myself at him. His rule about courting before sex be damned.

"My mom had a substance abuse problem."

"Had? I'm sorry you lost her."

I chuckle but there's nothing amusing about my mom. "I didn't lose her. She didn't die. She kicked me out when I was seventeen and I haven't seen nor heard from her since. Ironic since if she knew I had a good job she'd be on my front porch begging for money for drugs."

Barney growls, and it feels as if all the oxygen is being sucked from the room. "She kicked you out? She left a vulnerable seventeen-year-old on the streets?"

"I was fine. I survived."

"No, honey, you didn't survive. You thrived."

Goosebumps explode on my skin at his words. He's not feeding me some line to get me in his bed. Um, hello, I'm already in his bed. He moves forward until he's sitting at my hip. He lays his hand on my stomach before asking, "What happened?"

"I went to her to complain about her husband making me feel uncomfortable, and she accused me of trying to seduce my step-father."

His hand spasms. "Did your step-father abuse you?"

I pat his hand. "No, but he was the king of creepy. He was always leering at my breasts, and I caught him once in my bedroom sniffing my underwear." I shiver.

"And now you've sworn off relationships because of him?"

I drop my gaze to the comforter. "Not exactly."

Barney inches closer until he's near enough to palm my cheeks. "If this is too difficult, you don't need to tell me more. I would never make you re-live a painful time in your life."

Those are exactly the right words to form the key to unlock the past. My mouth opens and I wave my dirty laundry in his face.

"My mother was married four times by the time I left home. Each time the guy started out great. He would bring me candy or books or give me a little spending money. But each time – each and every time – once he was married to my mom, he'd change. He'd become a lazy asshole who treated my mom like trash and expected me to be his personal servant. Marriage changes people. They become jerks."

"Then, it's marriage you have a problem with and not relationships?"

"Well, yeah, but relationships lead to marriage." It's a slippery slope, and I have no intention of putting spikes on my shoes – talk about unattractive footwear – to stop myself from slipping and sliding down the slope.

"Alrighty then. We just won't get married."

My brow wrinkles. "You want to live in sin with me?" Wait. He never said he wanted to live with me at all. *Talk about jumping the gun, Val.* "I mean, it's …"

He kisses my forehead. "I don't give a shit about living in sin. You don't want to get married. We don't get married."

"You sound like it's a foregone conclusion."

"Honey, it is a foregone conclusion. You need to catch up is all."

"But, living in sin. Aren't you worried about going to hell?" I'm grasping at straws now.

The spark in his eyes dies. "No, honey, I'm not. The things I've done… They may have been sanctioned by the U.S. government, but they definitely weren't sanctioned by anyone's god."

I set the breakfast tray on the ground so I can throw my arms around him and hug him tight. "I'm sorry. I shouldn't have said anything. I wasn't thinking."

He buries his face in my shoulder for a few moments before taking a deep breath and lifting his head. "There's nothing for you to be sorry about." He smirks. "And since I now know your problem isn't with relationships." He kisses my shoulder. "We can return to our previously scheduled activities." His tongue licks a path from my shoulder to my ear before nibbling on my earlobe.

"But I didn't say I'm your woman," I pant.

"You will. Don't you worry. You will." He winks before his head descends and his lips find mine.

He's not wrong. Fifteen minutes later, I'm willing to tell him whatever he wants to hear – including how I'm willing to give a relationship with him a try.

Chapter 27

Even if there wasn't gravity on earth, I'd still fall for you.

I'm curled into Barney on the sofa on Wednesday night when there's a loud knock on the door. Barney immediately goes on full alert. His body tightens before he springs to his feet, draws a weapon out of nowhere, and prowls to the door. His body relaxes after he peers through the peephole.

"Your girl gang is here," he says over his shoulder before hiding the weapon again and opening the door.

Faith rushes in followed by Chrissie, Hailey, Phoebe, Suzie, and Lexi. "Someone's mighty cozy on their couch."

I roll my eyes before standing. "What are you doing here?"

"The question is – what are you doing here? Why aren't you in your apartment?"

Suzie snorts. "Duh. Because she's canoodling with Barney on his sofa."

"Ms. I Don't Do Relationships is canoodling with a man on his sofa in his house? Have we entered the Twilight Zone?" Faith asks.

Phoebe holds up her hand. "I don't care where we are as long as there's a bathroom."

Barney points to the bathroom, and she rushes off as fast as she can in her high heels, which is surprisingly fast considering she's pregnant and her heels are sky high.

Faith points to Barney. "You need to leave so we can talk about you."

He crosses his arms over his chest. "I'm not leaving Val alone."

"Ha! There is something going on." Faith crosses her arms over her chest. "Are you in danger? What happened? Did you get in trouble in Saint Louis? Are you on the lam?"

"On the lam?" Suzie's eyes widen. "As in running from the police? This is going to be fun."

Hailey hits her shoulder. "Now you know the proper definition of a term?"

Faith ignores them and stomps over to me. "What's going on?"

Lexi clears her throat. "Who votes Val can have her secrets?"

Chrissie's hand shoots into the air and Phoebe shouts "Me!" through the bathroom door.

Suzie slaps Chrissie's hand out of the air. Or she tries. Chrissie is over half a foot taller than her. She jumps up and down to reach Chrissie's hand with no effect.

"I veto your vote and since Val's my best friend my veto overrules your vote," Faith announces.

"Is this a rule?" Suzie asks. "Or is she making up friendship rules?"

Faith rips the blanket off of me. "Get up. We're going out. It's girl's night out."

"It's Wednesday, and I have to work tomorrow," I protest.

"Don't care." She tugs me off the couch and shoves me toward the bathroom. "Get changed. We're going."

Phoebe walks out of the bathroom and captures my hands. "You don't need to tell us your secrets, but a night out won't hurt anyone."

"Fine," I mutter before stomping off to find some clothes to change into.

By the time I come out of the bathroom fifteen

minutes later – I don't rush getting ready for a night out for anyone – Lenny is standing in the kitchen with Barney.

I point to Lenny. "What's he doing here?"

"He's on you tonight," Barney answers.

I frown. "You're not coming?"

"Your friends want to spend the night talking about me."

They do, which is why he needs to be there. They'll have to mind their manners with him around. He smirks as if he can read my mind. "You'll be safe with Lenny." He kisses my forehead before spinning me around and nudging me toward the door. "Now go before your friends explode with curiosity."

"It's not actually possible to explode with curiosity." I should know. I didn't know why Faith ran away from Saint Louis for a year and it didn't kill me to not know why, although it felt like it did at the time.

We pile into Lenny's SUV and drive to a wine bar downtown. The place is practically empty since it's Wednesday night and the after-work crowd has already left. We have no trouble finding a table with enough seats for our large group.

Lenny doesn't sit down. He's too busy playing bodyguard. Except his eyes don't rove the room for danger. Nope. They're too busy straying to Lexi every few seconds.

"Spill," Faith demands once we've ordered a bottle of wine.

"I'd much rather know why Lenny can't keep his eyes off Lexi."

Lexi's face flames as everyone directs their attention at her.

"Yeah, Lexi," Hailey pushes. "What's happening between you and my Uncle Lenny?"

Phoebe shoves her shoulder. "Leave Lexi alone. If she wants to keep her relationship with Lenny secret, let her."

Hailey snorts. "You're only backing her up because your date isn't until March."

Lexi's nose wrinkles in confusion. "Date? What do you mean?"

"They're betting on when you and Lenny will seal the deal," Chrissie explains.

"There will be no sealing of the deal," Lexi announces. Lenny, who's standing too far away to hear, whips his head in her direction and smirks. Guess he's not standing too far away after all.

"What's holding you back?" I ask.

The waitress arrives with our wine and some bubbly water for Phoebe and Suzie.

Suzie gulps her water and starts coughing and sneezing while fanning her face. "Bubbles. In my nose."

"You need to wait until the water stops fizzing before you drink it," Phoebe tells her. Her eyes widen when she realizes what she said and how she said it. "Sorry, I channeled my mother there for a second."

I want to ask Phoebe about her family. I know there's a story there. I mean I do know about her ex-husband being in jail for kidnapping her. It's public knowledge after all. But why did she cut off her family? I don't ask her, though. I'd be a hypocrite since I have no intention of ever telling another living soul about my mom.

Faith points to her watch while glaring at me. My brow furrows. "What?"

"Tick tock. Time's up. Time to tell us what's going on."

I lean back in my chair and cross my arms over my chest. "Like you told me about the gang in Saint Louis after Ollie?"

She grimaces. "Sorry. I was wrong. I should have told you, but I was scared."

I cock an eyebrow. As if being scared is an excuse for not telling your best friend why you disappeared in the middle of the night?

A Valentine for Valerie

Phoebe pats my hand. "You don't have to tell us if you don't want to." She glares at Chrissie. "Some people aren't good with letting friends in."

Chrissie rolls her eyes. "I explained I am not at liberty to tell you what happened."

"It's true," Lexi chimes in.

Hailey narrows her eyes on Lexi. "But you know what happened?"

Lexi doesn't respond. She simply stares back at Hailey with a blank look on her face.

Suzie gasps. "Holy macaroni! Chrissie and Lexi know each other 'from work'."

Hailey sighs. "Air quotes are for euphemisms. They did work together."

Suzie ignores Hailey and leans close to whisper. "Are you both super-secret soldiers like Wally?"

"Is it really super-secret if you know about it?" Chrissie asks instead of answering her question.

Faith slams a hand down on the table and the wine glasses rattle. I scoop mine up before it can fall over. "Enough! Stop distracting from the matter at hand."

I raise my hand. "What's the matter at hand?"

"Smart ass." Faith scowls. "Are you in danger?"

This one I'll answer. "Barney seems to think I am. I disagree."

"Why does Barney think you're in danger?"

I shrug. "Because his go-to response is overreaction?" Oops. I shouldn't have made my statement sound like a question.

"What. Happened?"

"I don't want to talk about it."

Faith tilts her head and studies me until I start to squirm. She smirks. "Okay. We can talk about why you and Barney were snuggled—"

"Canoodling!" Suzie corrects.

Faith clears her throat. "Why you and Barney were canoodling on his couch when we arrived."

"And why you haven't slept in your apartment since Saturday," Hailey adds.

"How do you know where I've been sleeping?"

She frowns. "Don't insult me."

"I withdraw my question," I tell her.

"Does this place sell tequila?" is Hailey's bizarre response. "We'll do a few shots and she'll talk then."

Chrissie cocks an eyebrow. "Like you got me to talk after a few shots?"

Hailey waves a hand at her in dismissal. "Valerie's not some super-secret spy like you. Plus, she's at least four inches shorter than me. I got this."

"And to think, I was worried about making friends when I moved here," Lexi says.

Lenny's head whips toward her and he smiles. She tucks her chin into her chest, but not before I notice the blush on her cheeks.

Faith clasps my hands and bats her eyelashes at me. "Come on, Val. I admit I was wrong not to tell you about the gang situation. Don't shut me out because I was stupid. If you can't tell me why Barney thinks you're in danger, can you at least promise me you'll consider giving the man a chance?"

I put on a frown. "Sorry, I can't promise you that."

Her shoulders fall. "I know your childhood was a complete and total shitshow, but isn't it time to let it go? Don't give the bitch any more power over you."

She's right. I shouldn't allow my mother to have any power over me. She's also wrong. It's not time to let it go. It's past time.

"Sorry. I can't let it go now." I pause for dramatic effect. "Because I already did."

Her eyebrows nearly fly off her forehead. "You mean…"

"Yep. I'm giving the lug a chance."

She screams and wraps her arms around me. It's awkward as hell since we're sitting across from each other at the table, but I don't care.

"Champagne!" Hailey shouts. "We need champagne!"

I release Faith and survey the other women at the table. Everyone's smiling at me because they're happy for me. This is what I was missing in Saint Louis. People to have my back. Following Faith to Milwaukee was the right thing to do. I'm certain of it.

Chapter 28

You must be a broom because you've swept me off my feet.

"And then I said to him, I don't know where your chicken is but this is my chicken," Lexi finishes her story and I burst out laughing.

When I manage to get myself under control, I glance toward the door to watch as Barney strolls in. Confession. I love to watch the man walk. He might be the jokester of the brothers, but when he walks it's clear as day how much power he holds in his body. Trust me. I know firsthand how much power his body harnesses. I bite my lip as he prowls toward me and he smirks in response.

He leans down and kisses me. "Have a good time?" he asks against my lips.

Faith claps. "I love this! My best friend is falling in love with a brother of my soon-to-be-husband. Life is awesome!" Good thing this place is empty since she screamed the last bit.

I roll my eyes at her. "It's a bit early to talk about love."

Chrissie giggles. "I said the exact same thing!" She wiggles her left hand at me, and her diamond ring sparkles. "I was wrong. You go, girl."

Barney chuckles. "Chrissie is coming into her girl power," I tell him.

Lenny clears his throat. "All right, ladies. Time to go." He pulls Lexi's chair out for her and she glares up at him.

"I'm perfectly capable of standing on my own." She stands and wobbles. Lenny reaches an arm out to steady her, but she bats him away. "No touching the merchandise, mister."

Lenny's eyes flash with pain before he smirks. "If you fall and break your nose, it won't be my fault."

"I'm not going to fall. I'll have you know I was brought up on moonshine. Have you ever drunk moonshine?"

Chrissie groans. "I have. The stuff should be illegal."

"It is," Lexi whisper-shouts. "My family thinks laws are merely advisory."

"It's settled!" Hailey claps and Suzie who was dozing using the table as a pillow wakes up.

"What? What's going on?" She looks around the room as if she doesn't know how she got here. She should have left with Phoebe when Ryker came to pick up his wife, but she has an awful case of fear of missing out.

"Lexi is going to procure us some moonshine," Hailey explains.

"Isn't moving an illegal substance across a state line a federal offense?" Faith asks.

Lenny wipes a hand down his face. "It's like wrangling cats," he mutters.

"Cats are awesome," Chrissie says. "I have a little kitten. Her name is Gray."

"I'm a dog person," Hailey says as she walks toward the door. She motions to Lenny. "Come on, Lenny. Quit lallygagging. I'm ready to go home."

Lenny rounds up the rest of the women and herds them toward the door.

"I'll pay the bill," Barney says.

"Phoebe gave the bartender her credit card before she left."

When I tried to protest, she shushed me. As if shushing me has any effect. But then Ryker told me to let it go. And I admit when the big bad bounty hunter gives me orders, I tend to listen. Besides, Phoebe has money to burn. If she wants to treat her friends to a night out, who am I to complain?

Barney helps me into my coat before putting his arm over my shoulders and leading me outside.

"Holy balls, it's cold out here."

He hurries me into the truck before slamming my door and rushing around the hood. After he switches on the vehicle, he aims the vents my way and increases the heat until it's blaring warmth at me.

"We don't have to live in Milwaukee if you don't want to," he says as he drives out of the parking lot.

My mouth gapes open. "What? You would leave the city where all your brothers and their families are?"

He reaches over the console to rest his hand on my thigh. "For you, I would."

He's talking crazy. He's known me two months and he's willing to leave his family for me? What's a word stronger than crazy? Because that's what Barney is.

"Honey, we're home," Barney whispers.

I jolt awake. "What?" I must have fallen asleep on the drive. It's been a long day on top of a few tough days. Add in the wine and I'm surprised I didn't fall asleep next to Suzie at the wine bar.

He opens my door and lifts me out. "I can walk."

"In those shoes?" He points at my high-heeled boots.

"Whatever." I'm not going to fight about a man carrying me across an icy parking lot. I can be gracious. I mean, I think I can. Just because I've never done it before doesn't mean I'm incapable.

We settle into our nighttime routine. I use the bathroom while Barney 'closes down'. Whatever that means. Once I'm finished, I crawl into bed while he uses the bathroom. There's a bottle of water and two aspirin on the nightstand on my side of the bed.

I swallow the aspirin and put the bottle of water

back on my nightstand. Whoa. Hold up, Val. *My side of the bed? My nightstand?* You don't live here. You're staying here until the situation at work is settled. This is not your new home.

Except when I study the loft, I have a hard time believing myself. My clothes are in the dresser with my jewelry spread across the top. A book I'm reading is on the nightstand. My shoes are lined up next to Barney's at the door. And my jackets are hanging there, too. My sewing machine is sitting atop the kitchen table surrounded by pieces of fabric I'm working on.

Everywhere I glance, I spot a piece of me. Barney even bought the coffee machine I have. Or used to have. Mine was destroyed. What am I doing? I know I told Barney I'd give us being in a relationship a chance, but all the signs point to us having moved in together.

We need to slow down. I should probably leave. Find somewhere else to stay until the 'danger' is gone. I'm not convinced there is any danger. Nothing's happened since last week and my boss is acting as if everything is normal at work. Except for staring at my roses. I can't blame him. They are very pretty.

Barney climbs into bed and draws me near. I fight him, but my efforts are futile. He doesn't budge. "This is a bad idea."

He freezes. "What is?"

"Me being here with you. Look around. It's like I've moved in."

"Yeah, and?"

"And?" I screech. "And we barely know each other. We went from you going hot and cold on me to me living with you. It's too quick."

He sighs. "I'm sorry I was hot and cold with you. I'm sorry I hurt you. But I promise you, no more cold. I—" He clears his throat. "I care about you. I won't run away again."

Did he almost say he loves me? *Nope. Val. We are not thinking about the L-word.* Talk about a tizzy waiting to happen.

"I believe you," I say instead. "But this is all too soon."

He grunts. "I disagree, but the point is mute now anyway."

"You better not be saying my opinion doesn't matter, buster," I grumble.

"Of course, your opinion matters. I meant you are staying here until the danger passes. We can talk about where we live afterwards."

"Where *we* live afterwards? Were you trying to slide that by me?"

He shrugs. "Maybe."

"You know I'm proud of you," he murmurs into my hair.

This conversation is giving me whiplash. "What? What are you talking about?"

"I know it must have been difficult for you to tell your friends about us being serious."

I elbow him. "I never agreed to us being serious."

"Okay, honey. Okay."

"Don't placate me."

"Sorry, I'm tired." He yawns to demonstrate. "It's been a long day and you need to get up in six hours, so you have an hour to spend in the bathroom farting around doing whatever it is you do in there."

"What I do is make myself presentable. It's not easy when your age starts with a four. Everything starts to sag and wrinkles appear overnight."

He rolls us so he's lying on top of me. "Honey, you're gorgeous. You're gorgeous right now with all your make-up cleaned away, and you're gorgeous after spending an hour curling your hair and putting on make-up."

I roll my eyes. "There's no need to give me pretty words. I'm already in bed with you." I wrap my legs around his waist and arch my back to rub myself against him. His cock twitches and I wiggle my eyebrows at him. "There are other things we could be doing right now."

"You're going to bitch and moan at me when I have to wake you in the morning."

"But it's worth it."

He grins. "Yeah, it is."

His lips crash to mine and he proceeds to show me I'm right. It's worth losing a bit of sleep to have my world rocked by this man.

Chapter 29

Do you have a bandage? Because I scraped my knee falling for you.

Barney

I kiss Val's forehead, and she swats me away. "Five more minutes."

I wave the coffee cup under her nose, and she sighs. It's the same sound she makes when I slide into her. My pants tighten at the memories those thoughts bring. I clear my throat before I decide to hell with her work and climb back into her bed with her.

"Honey, you need to get up now or you'll be late."

"Need sleep."

I chuckle at her grumpiness. "I guess next time it's late, we'll go to sleep instead of having sex."

Her eyes fly open, and she glares at me. "You're cruel."

I hand her the coffee cup. "Got you to open your eyes, didn't I?"

She gulps her coffee before setting the cup on the nightstand and rolling out of bed. She groans as she stands.

"How bad is your hangover?"

"I've had worse," she says as she lumbers to the bathroom. Wait for it. Five. Four. Three. Two. One. "Holy cheeseballs!"

I chuckle at her reaction to seeing her reflection in the mirror. I don't care how her hair is mussed up from my hands running through it while I made love to her last night. I love her. She's always beautiful to me.

I nearly told her I loved her last night. I managed to bite my tongue before the words came out, though. Val's already freaking about living here with me – and make no mistake about it, she is living with me from now on. She isn't going back to her ratty apartment.

After we settled down to sleep, I waited for the panic to come. I haven't been involved with a woman since Ruby died. I haven't wanted to be. But when no panic came, I realized I'm finally moving on from what happened to Ruby. I still feel guilty, but the guilt isn't weighing me down like it was just a few short months ago.

I prepare a breakfast sandwich for Valerie while she gets ready. She's not going to have time to eat before we leave, but I won't let her begin her day without some food in her stomach. She needs the energy to keep up with her job.

We're in my truck on the way to her office an hour later. I hand her the sandwich and she sighs in relief.

"Are you on me all day?" she asks after she swallows the first bite.

"Until noon. Then, Sid takes over."

"Will you have time for lunch before you leave?"

"Trouble, are you suggesting a little afternoon delight?" I wink at her.

"No, but now you mention it..."

I chuckle as I slow down for a yellow light. I glance into the rearview mirror and notice the car behind me isn't slowing down. I scan the intersection, but the cross-traffic is already moving. I have to stop, or we'll end up sideswiped the second the truck crosses the stop line.

I throw an arm across Valerie's chest. "Hold on. This is going to be rough."

Before the truck has come to a complete stop, the car behind us rams into us. Valerie falls to the side and her head hits the window.

"Valerie!" I shout. I keep one eye on the car behind us. It's backing up to ram into us again. I can't let it hit us again, but I'm trapped. If I drive forward, I'll be driving straight into traffic.

"Valerie! We need to get out of here, now!"

She doesn't respond. Not even a groan. I give up on keeping an eye on the car to concentrate on Val. The side window is cracked from where she hit it and there's blood trailing down her face.

I hear a squeal before the car behind us whips around to pass us as the light switches to green. Shit. I need to follow, but Val's hurt. I need to care for her. She's my first priority.

The sound of my phone ringing sounds loud in the cabin. "What?" I bark.

"I'm on the car. Take Val to the hospital." When I don't answer Chrissie right away, she continues, "I promise you, Barney. I will capture whoever is in the car. You look after Val. She needs you right now."

She doesn't wait for me to thank her before she hangs up. Less than a second later, her car flies by chasing the car that hit us. I don't know what she's doing out here this morning, but I'm not going to worry about it right now. I've got to get Val to the hospital.

I drive as fast as I can to the hospital. The whole time I shout Val's name. By the time I arrive at the emergency room entrance, I'm begging Val to wake up. She hasn't made a sound since she hit the window. I can feel the panic bubbling up inside me. It's a grenade sitting in my stomach ticking away.

I skid to a stop, but I don't bother to switch off the engine as I jump out of my door and run to Valerie. I want to lift her into my arms, but I know better.

"Help!" I shout toward the emergency room. "My wife is unresponsive."

A team runs out of the entrance with a stretcher. They put a cervical collar on her before lowering her onto the stretcher and wheeling her into the hospital. I follow them, but one of the nurses stops me when we reach a room.

"You need to let us do our job," she says and closes the door behind her.

I debate throwing the door open anyway for several seconds in the hallway. When someone places a hand on my shoulder, I whirl around with my fists raised. Sid retreats with his hands out in front of him.

"Didn't mean to startle you, brother."

I lower my hands.

"You'll only be in the way," he says.

"But she's all alone." The words are ripped from me. I don't want her to be alone. There's nothing worse than waking up injured, not knowing where you are and how you got there.

"Come on. You need to fill out *your wife's* paperwork."

He's baiting me about the wife part. He can tease me all he wants. Val doesn't want to be my wife because she doesn't believe in marriage, but she doesn't realize Wisconsin has common law marriage. She'll be as good as my wife in a few years.

While I'm finishing up with the paperwork, Max and Faith arrive. Faith stomps toward me. "Where is she? What happened? Is she okay?"

I have no reassurances to give her. "We're waiting to hear."

She collapses into Max's arms. "I knew she was in danger," she cries. "I knew it! But she wouldn't tell me anything." She glares at me.

"It's work related. She doesn't want to lose her job."

It's more than Valerie would want me to say, but I don't care right now. The only thing I care about is her being okay.

We find seats in the waiting room. I sit for approximately two seconds before I spring to my feet and start pacing the area. I rub the back of my neck with my hand as I walk back and forth through the room. Five minutes pass. Then, ten minutes and still no news. When fifteen minutes have passed, I'm done waiting. I march to the desk.

"Do you have any news about Valerie Cook?" I demand.

The nurse frowns at me before typing into her computer. "She's being taken for an MRI."

"Has she woken up? Can I go with her?"

"I don't know and no."

"She's alone. She'll be disorientated."

The nurse takes pity on me. "I'll call you as soon as I know anything."

"She's getting an MRI," I tell Max, Faith, and Sid when I return to my pacing of the waiting room.

Sid stands. "Come on. Let's get a coffee."

"I don't want a coffee," I say without looking at him.

"Yeah, you do," he says in a voice that has me looking at him. He has news.

"Coffee sounds good."

As soon as we're around the corner and out of hearing range from the waiting room, I demand, "Did Chrissie get him?"

He nods. "Wally and Chrissie are with him now."

The news doesn't relieve me. It inflames me. "Who the hell was it and what did he want?"

Sid chuckles. "Between Chrissie and Wally, he confessed to everything he's ever done wrong since he was in diapers within minutes."

I believe it. Chrissie is ex-CIA and Wally – well, Wally is something else entirely. Suzie and Hailey aren't far off when they call him a super-secret soldier.

"He's a soldier in Sturgess' organization."

My heart stops. This is exactly what I've been afraid of for the past week. "Did Sturgess order a hit on Valerie?"

"Not a hit. He was only supposed to scare her."

Fuck! "Is he willing to testify against Sturgess?"

His grin stretches from ear to ear. "He's singing about all kinds of stuff. Including how Val's boss, Mr. Davenport, is an intricate part of the organization."

"What's Aiden say?"

"He's working with the DA to procure arrest warrants for Joseph Sturgess and Daniel Davenport as we speak."

I sag against the wall. "Then, it's over. Val's safe."

"Mr. Lewis?" The nurse motions me toward her. I race down the hall.

"What is it? Is Valerie okay? Did something happen?"

"She's being moved into a room upstairs. I can escort you there now."

"A room? What's wrong with her?"

"I don't have any information on her condition. Would you like me to take you upstairs?"

I nod. I glance back at Sid over my shoulder. He motions me forward. "We'll be right behind you."

Of course, they will. My brothers would never leave me in a time of need. And with Val injured, I need them now more than ever.

Chapter 30

If I were a transplant surgeon, I'd give you my heart.

Barney

I drop my head to the mattress next to where my hand is clutching Val's. Her hand is limp in mine. It's been hours, and she still hasn't woken up. The MRI showed there was no swelling in the brain, but she remains unconscious. The doctors can't tell me why. All they say is not to panic, her body is healing itself.

How can I not panic? She's never this still. Even when she's sleeping, Val is alive. She kicks and mumbles in her sleep. And I, the selfish asshole that I am, found it annoying. Now, I'd do anything to hear her mumble a word or kick her covers off.

"Wake up, honey," I beg her. "Please, wake up."

The door squeaks as it opens, and I whip my head up to check on who's entering. I know Valerie is safe. Her boss and Joseph Sturgess are behind bars. But with her laying here vulnerable, I need to remain vigilant. She wouldn't want anyone to see her this way.

"It's us," Faith says as she strolls in holding Max's hand.

"Any change?" Max asks.

I grunt 'no' before my gaze returns to Val. She's breathing on her own and a multitude of machines beep away telling me her vital signs are good. Then, why isn't she awake?

Max squeezes my shoulder. "Come on. You need a break."

I shake him off. "I'm not leaving her alone."

Faith stands on the other side of the bed. "I'll stay with her."

"Let's go. Faith has her," Max orders, but my body is frozen. I can't leave her.

"What if she wakes up and I'm not here?"

He doesn't understand. He doesn't know how all the other men in her life have let her down. I won't let Val believe I'm one of those men. I may screw up, but I will never let her down.

"You need a break, brother. Have you even moved for the past hours?"

"Doesn't matter," I grumble. I don't give the first fuck about my needs. All that matters right here right now is her.

"Brother."

I glare at him. "Don't brother me. If it were Faith laying in this bed, you'd say the same thing I'm saying now. I'm not leaving her."

"And you'd be standing here reminding me I need a break, or I'll be too wrecked to care for Faith when she wakes."

I don't bother responding. I don't lie to my brothers and telling him he's way off base would be a lie.

"Five minutes to stretch your legs, get a bite to eat and drink something. Then, you can come back here refreshed."

"Three minutes and we're not leaving the hallway outside of her room," I negotiate.

He nods. My body protests when I stand, but I hide my wince from Max. I lean over Val and kiss her cheek. "I'll be back in a few minutes, honey."

I hold my breath and wait for her response. Usually, when I kiss her, her breath hitches. There's no response now, though.

I follow Max into the hallway to find Sid and Lenny waiting on me. "If this is some kind of intervention, you need to back off."

Sid holds out a cup of coffee and a sandwich. "No intervention. Just taking your pulse. Checking you're okay."

I ignore his outstretched hand. "How the hell do you expect me to be okay? The woman I love is lying unconscious in a hospital bed."

A smile lights up Sid's face. "'Bout damn time you got over Ruby."

I open my mouth to lash out at him for mentioning Ruby. It's my standard practice when my wife's name is mentioned, but my mouth falls closed when I realize the anger I usually feel at being reminded of how I failed her isn't there.

Sid slaps my shoulder. "Happy for you, brother."

"Are we done? I need to get back."

"It's been thirty seconds," Max responds.

"Don't care."

Sid shoves the coffee in my hand. "Drink some coffee at least."

My hand automatically lifts, and I gulp at the scolding liquid. When he tries to hand me the sandwich, I refuse. The idea of eating has my stomach clenching in protest.

The corridor door swings open and Wally strolls over to us. "Thank you," I tell him as soon as he's in hearing range.

"Not me you need to thank. My wife sat outside your building all night last night."

My brow wrinkles. "All night?"

He frowns. "She swore she saw someone waiting for you outside of the wine bar last night."

"And you let her sit outside Barney's building all night?" Lenny asks.

He crosses his arms over his chest. "I promised her when I married her I wouldn't change who she is and I'd respect her skills."

Wally never had a serious relationship until he met Chrissie. The moment he saw her, his bachelor days were a thing of the past. Apparently, he's learned a thing or two about being in a relationship, though.

Max cocks his eyebrow. "And you didn't sit in another car all night making sure she was safe?"

Wally shrugs. Maybe he hasn't learned anything about relationships after all.

"Thank Chrissie for me, will ya?"

"Thank her yourself. As soon as Val's awake, the women will descend on the hospital. Chrissie's holding them off until then."

Aiden chuckles as he joins us. "Chrissie has her job cut out for her. Hailey's chomping at the bit to rush down here."

"Val wouldn't want anyone to see her like this." I turn to Max. "Can you have Faith—"

"Already done. We stopped by your place before we came back and picked up some clothes and other stuff Val will need when she wakes."

When she wakes? Will she wake? Night is falling. She's been out all day. I don't know how much longer I can hold it together. She needs to wake up. My chin falls to my chest, and I stare at the ugly ass flooring as I try to force those thoughts back in the box in my mind where I shoved them this morning.

Max's hand squeezes my shoulder. "She'll wake up, brother. Have a little faith."

I feel my eyes itch with tears for the first time since Ruby died. I take a deep breath and force those tears back where they belong. When I manage the herculean task, I discover my brothers are surrounding me; making sure my moment of weakness remains private.

"Thanks." I don't need to tell them what I'm thanking them for. They know.

Someone clears her throat and I glance over my shoulder to find Sid's wife, Mary Ann, waving at me. "I don't mean to interrupt…"

Sid breaks rank to pull her to him. He kisses her hair. "Thanks for coming."

She wrings her hands. "I'm afraid I'm not much help. I'm not a doctor."

"What's going on?" I ask.

"I asked Mary Ann to review Val's record."

He doesn't need to explain further. He knows the fear I live with. The fear of not knowing the truth about Val's condition. Thus far, the doctors appear to be open with me since they think Val is my wife. But it doesn't erase the fear coursing through my veins. Not since Ruby hid her medical condition from me until it was too late.

"I'm sorry, Barney," Mary Ann tells me. "There's nothing in her file to explain why she's still unconscious. The doctors aren't lying. There isn't any swelling in her brain. Which is good. Very good. She can wake up anytime."

I didn't realize how terrified I was of the unknown until the relief hits me. There isn't a reason for Val's condition the doctors are hiding from me. Thank my lucky stars.

I kiss Mary Ann's cheek. "Thank you."

She beams up at me. "Anytime, Barney. Anytime." She squeezes my hand. "She's going to be all right. Val is tough."

Damn straight she is. And she's all mine.

"I'm going back in."

"At least take the sandwich and pretend you're going to eat it," Sid says and shoves the thing in my hands. "Mary Ann made it for you."

I grab the sandwich I have no intention of eating and push the door to Val's room open. When Faith looks at me, I notice tears running down her face. I rush to Val's side.

"What happened?" My heart constricts in my chest and I fight to force oxygen into my lungs.

"You love Valerie?"

"Of course, I love Val. What happened?" I repeat my question as I squeeze Val's hand and scan her body for any change in her condition.

"Nothing happened. I'm happy for my best friend is all. She's finally getting her happily ever after."

Max sighs as he wraps his arms around his fiancée. I avert my gaze before the jealousy can hit and I say something extremely stupid.

"You'll have this, brother," Max says. "You'll have this."

I hope to hell he's right. Please, Val, wake the hell up.

Chapter 31

Let's commit the perfect crime together. I'll steal your heart and you can steal mine.

I groan and try to lift my hand to rub my aching head, but my hand refuses to move. Dang. This hangover is going to be hell.

"Val, honey," Barney whispers. "Open your eyes."

Open my eyes? Why would I open my eyes? Experience tells me opening my eyes is not going to make me feel better.

"Five more minutes," I mumble.

"Come on, honey," he coaxes. "Let me look into those gorgeous blue eyes of yours. I miss them."

Miss them? How long have I been asleep? I groan. I'm late for work, aren't I? Shit. Mr. Davenport is going to lose his mind. My phone is probably smoking with all his messages by now.

I inhale a deep breath and open my eyes. Or, more accurately, I try to. The stupid things aren't cooperating.

"There you go, honey."

My eyes flutter open to find Barney hovering over me. His eyes close as he mutters, "thank fucking god."

"Why are you thanking god? You're acting weird." I try to look around, but the room is dark. "It's still dark out. Why did you wake me up? I want to sleep more."

"Hang on, honey. Wait for the doctors to come in and check on you."

I wrinkle my brow in confusion. Shit. That hurts. "Doctors? What are you talking about?"

He freezes. "You don't remember this morning?"

I think back. This morning? Did he wake me with breakfast in bed? No, that was Tuesday. Today's Wednesday.

"I think I drank too much at girls' night out," I say instead of answering his question.

"Do you know what day it is?"

"It's Wednesday morning. Can you stop being weird and tell me why you said the word doctors?"

He squeezes my hand. "It's Wednesday night. Technically, it's Thursday morning."

"Thursday morning? You're not making any sense. You didn't let me sleep all day, did you? I'll lose my job. Please tell me you at least called in sick for me."

My voice feels scratchy and I cough. Barney places a straw in my mouth. "Small sips."

I do as he says, but only because I'm confused as to what's going on here. What the hell did I drink to cause me to lose an entire day of my life?

I nod to indicate I'm done drinking and he removes the straw and places the cup on the side table. Wait. This isn't Barney's side table. I blink my eyes to adjust to the low lightening before I scan the room. This isn't Barney's place. I try to sit up, but Barney is there keeping me in the bed.

"Where are we? What's happening?" My heart pounds as the panic rises.

"We were in an accident. A car rear-ended us while I was driving you to work this morning."

"We were in a car accident?" I screech.

"I'm sorry. I didn't protect you," is Barney's bizarre answer.

"Someone has a god complex. You can't control every single car and driver on the road, you know."

"I should have realized we were being followed. I should have paid better attention."

Better attention? Being followed? The memory of being at a red light pops up and I remember Barney reaching across the truck and trying to protect me before a car hit us and then ... I don't know what happened after the sound of metal on metal. I have no recollection.

"You hit your head on the window and were knocked unconscious," Barney explains.

"How long have I been out?"

"Sixteen hours, fourteen minutes, and approximately thirty-two seconds."

My eyes widen at his response. His answer is pretty damn exact. "Have you been here the entire time?"

At his nod, I notice his appearance. His clothes are wrinkled, his hair is a mess as if he's been running his hands through it all day, his eyes are bloodshot, and he has black smudges underneath his eyes.

"But what about your injuries? You were in the vehicle with me."

"I'm fine," he claims but I notice he winces when he settles himself in the chair.

I narrow my eyes at him. "You are not fine. You're hurt. Let me call the nurse to examine you."

Before I can press the call button, Barney's there. His hands frame my face. "I promise. I'm fine. My back is a little sore from sitting in the most uncomfortable chair in the world all day, but otherwise, I'm fine. I will never lie to you about my health. Never."

My hands latch onto his, and I squeeze. "Okay. I believe you."

The door opens, and a doctor breezes in. "Sleeping beauty is awake."

He proceeds with a physical exam, which involves a bunch of me telling him inane things a toddler would know such as what day of the week it is, what year it is, and how many fingers he's holding up. When he finally finishes and flips the chart closed, he smiles at me.

"You've suffered a severe concussion, Mrs. Cook,

but with some rest and relaxation, you'll be fine. I want you to stay at the hospital another day to make sure you're recovered before going home."

Another day? I sigh. "I need to get to work."

Barney's hand spasms in mine. "What?"

"I'll tell you in the morning."

I wait for the doctor to leave before I confront him. "You're telling me now, dude. What's going on?"

"Your boss is in jail."

My mouth drops open. I'm probably catching flies as I stare at him waiting for the punchline. There's always a punchline with Barney. But not this time.

"You're not kidding."

"I'm afraid not. Mr. Davenport was an intricate part of Joseph Sturgess' criminal enterprise."

I shiver. "Holy cow. I worked for that slimeball." Barney squeezes my hand, and I realize he's bracing himself. "There's more, isn't there?"

"Yeah." He swallows before telling me everything. How Sturgess had one of his men follow me and destroy my apartment and rear-end us. I'm shaking by the time he finishes. Barney crawls into the bed with me.

"You can't be in here with me. We're in a hospital," I protest.

"I don't care. I'm not standing by while the woman I love shakes in fear."

The woman he loves? "What did you say?" I croak.

"I love you, Valerie Cook." His lips meet mine in the briefest of kisses. "I'm never letting you go."

I open my mouth to remind him how we barely know each other. But those aren't the words that spill out of my mouth. "Barney Lewis, you did not just tell me you love me for the first time in a hospital!"

He chuckles. "Pretend I didn't say anything. I'll find another way to say I love you for the first time. Something romantic."

My heart decides galloping out of my chest is a good idea. I fight to breathe. I want to enjoy how his arms envelop me as he declares his love for me, but I can't. I know this is the beginning of the end. This is how things always started with my mom's boyfriends. All roses and butterflies until the L-word was spoken. Then, the men always changed. Always.

Barney growls. "Don't you fucking dare compare me to those men."

"How do you know what I'm thinking?"

He doesn't bother to respond to my question. He pinches my chin. "Look at me. I'm not going anywhere. You are stuck with me. If my brothers couldn't get me to leave your hospital room, you don't have a chance in hell."

His brothers tried to get him to leave? And he wouldn't? Of course, he didn't. He knew how long I'd been unconscious down to the minute. He didn't leave at the first sign of trouble like Mom's boyfriends always did. He didn't raise his voice and yell at me for wasting his time at the hospital. He hasn't once tried to blame me for bringing danger into his life. He's the perfect man.

Shit. Do I love him? Barney was supposed to be a fun distraction while I adjusted to my new life in Milwaukee. Somehow he burrowed himself under his skin and planted himself there.

Barney kisses my forehead. "It's okay, honey. Get some sleep. We don't have to talk about this now. I know you must have a raging headache."

We don't have to talk about this now? He's not going to force me to say I love you back? And when I refuse, fly into a rage, and start throwing shit?

Any doubt left in my mind about how I feel for this man evaporates. I am in so much trouble. And I'm not talking about how I'm out of a job since my boss is a sleazebag who's in bed with criminals.

Chapter 32

When a penguin finds a mate, they stay with them for the rest of their life. Will you be my penguin?

I throw my legs off the bed, intent on having a shower and changing into normal clothes before I blow this popsicle station.

Barney stands between my legs to block my path. "I don't think this is a good idea."

I want to scream at his words. He's said this at least a million times already today.

"The doctor said I could go home today," I point out for the millionth and first time.

"You had a severe concussion."

"You don't need to remind me. I'm the one with the killer headache."

Barney frowns. "This is why you should stay here. How do we know your headache isn't masking another issue?"

Ah, shit. I'm such an idiot. His wife died of a brain tumor. Of course, he's worried. I forget this tall, strong, handsome man has a tender heart I need to handle with care.

I squeeze his hands. "They did an MRI yesterday morning. There is no damage to my brain."

"I'm sorry. It's …"

I cut his words off with a kiss. "I know," I say against his lips. "I understand. You don't have to apologize."

I wait for him to acknowledge my words with a nod before I waggle my eyebrows. "Now, are you going to help me shower or what?"

He smirks. "I can help you shower all right."

He lifts me and carries me to the attached bathroom. I slap his shoulders. "I can walk."

He sets me down in front of the vanity. When I get a look at my face in the mirror above the sink, I yelp. My appearance is downright scary. I knew my hair would be a mess, but I hadn't expected the bruising on my face.

"I look like I went five rounds with the heavyweight champion." He growls. "What? I'm not exactly a featherweight."

I have curves and I'm not ashamed of them. I'm not going to spend my life dieting and not enjoying life so I can wear a size or two less than I do now. No way. Life's too much fun and wine is too yummy.

"I don't like you hurting."

"Me either." I whirl away from the mirror. I don't need to see myself to shower. "You going to help wash my back, lover?"

I glide a nail down his chest, and he moans. "Stop tempting me. You're hurt."

Does he have to remind me I'm hurt every two seconds? It's getting annoying. "Untie this hideous hospital gown. You can pick out some clothes while I shower."

Fifteen minutes and zero hanky-panky later, I'm ready to leave. A nurse arrives with a wheelchair. She glares at me and points to it. If she thinks I'm going to fight her, she's wrong. I've seen movies, I know you always have to leave the hospital in a wheelchair. I'd rather leave than fight about a stupid wheelchair.

Barney kisses me. "I'll bring my truck around."

When we arrive at the hospital entrance, Barney's already parked there with the door open waiting for us. He lifts me out of the wheelchair and places me gently in his truck. "I'm not made of glass. I don't break easily."

He doesn't respond as he exits the hospital parking lot. I study the interior of the vehicle as he drives.

A Valentine for Valerie

"This isn't your truck."

"I bought it yesterday."

"Yesterday? I thought you were in the hospital with me all day." Did he lie? Was he not there?

He reaches across the seat and squeezes my hand. "I was with you all day. I sent Lenny to the dealer to trade my truck in and buy this one."

"Oh."

He squeezes my hand. "Yeah. Oh."

"I'm sorry my troubles caused you to have to replace your truck."

He shrugs. "I needed to replace it anyway. This one has side airbags."

I don't comment on the side airbags. I know enough about Barney the man to know he's going to be a bit overprotective for a while. I can deal. Until I can't. Then, I'll scream at him until he hears me. Considering how great our sex life is now, I can't wait to try make-up sex with him.

When we arrive at his apartment building, he repeats the whole carry me like I'm a damsel in distress thing. I protest but not too hard. If I'm honest, I am feeling a bit tired.

He sets me down on the sofa and covers me with a blanket. "What can I get you? Are you hungry? Thirsty?"

Maybe I can't deal with him being overprotective after all. "A glass of water, please," I say to give the man a task to perform.

I look around the place as he gets my water. His apartment appears different. There are pictures hung on the walls. The shelves next to the entertainment center now house a variety of knick-knacks. And there's a large chest of drawers set against the wall next to the bed. What's going on here?

Barney hands me a glass of water and settles on the sofa next to me. "Your place is different."

He clears his throat. "I wanted it to be more comfortable for you."

That's when I notice it. The pictures on the wall are copies of prints I used to have on my walls. "What's going on?"

"I don't want you to move back into your apartment."

"And you thought you'd make your apartment a copycat of mine?"

His cheeks flame. "I want my place to be our place. I want you to feel like this is your home. I want this to be your home."

He's crazy. We hardly know each other. "We've known each other for a minute."

He cradles my face with his hands. "I love you, Valerie. I don't need to know you for years to know what my heart feels. When you winked at my joke the first time we met on Thanksgiving, I knew you were trouble. And I've never been happier to find trouble."

I bite my tongue before I tell him I love him, too. I've never told a man I love him. I can barely manage to tell Faith I love her without choking on my words. I realized I love him less than a day ago. I need time to figure out how to say the words out loud.

"Living together is a big step," are the words to finally leave my lips. Lame, Val.

"We've been living together for a week already."

I snort. "A week? This is the honeymoon phase. Even my mom's boyfriends could behave for a week."

As soon as the words are out of my mouth, I regret them. Barney sucks in a breath and he takes all of the oxygen in the room with him. My head throbs. I'm such a bitch. Barney has shown me nothing but kindness and I repay him with venom.

"I'm sorry. I shouldn't compare you to my mom's boyfriends."

He releases his breath. "I get it. You've spent the past three decades protecting your heart. It's second nature for you to lash out whenever you're afraid."

I narrow my eyes at him. "I'm not afraid."

He smiles, and it lights up his eyes. "Of course, you are. It's okay. I'm scared, too."

I roll my eyes. "Yeah, right. You don't expect me to believe bad-ass Barney is scared of anything, do you?"

His eyes are sparkling now. "Bad-ass Barney? I think you should call me that when we're in bed."

"In your dreams," I mutter.

"I don't need to dream, honey. Not anymore. Everything I've always wanted, but didn't dare dream I could have, is right here in my arms."

I shove his shoulder. "Stop being corny."

He winks. "I'll get you used to hearing all the corny stuff."

Great. He's determined to tear down my walls. I study the changes he's made in the apartment. Crap. He's doing an awfully fine job already. Time to try a different tactic.

"This place screams bachelor pad. It's not exactly set up for more than one person to live here. What am I going to do when we fight? Storm off to the bathroom?"

"Huh. You may have a point. I'll put this place on the market tomorrow."

My eyes nearly bug out of my head. "I didn't mean for you to sell your place!"

He shrugs as if selling his place is no big deal. "We'll need a bigger place for the two of us. And an outside would be nice. Maybe a yard with enough room to have everyone over for a barbeque."

A yard. I've always wanted a yard. A big yard with a white picket fence. "We could get a dog."

"I'll ask Max where he got Pepper from. Do you like brown labs?"

Does he need to ask? "Everyone likes brown labs."

"We'll wait until we find a house before we adopt a

puppy. I don't want him getting used to this place and then have to move him to a new one."

My mouth is now hanging open. "You're serious, aren't you?"

"Damn straight, I am."

"What is it about you and your friends? You don't know how to take things slow, do you?"

He kisses my nose before answering. "We know what we want when we want it. And we know life is too damn short to screw around."

I cock an eyebrow. "Dating isn't screwing around."

"Oh, we're going to date," he says in a voice dripping with sin. "But you'll be living with me while it's happening."

I study his face. He's completely and totally serious. And I'm actually considering this. I do love him after all. Maybe us living together will show me he's the same as every other man I've ever known. Or maybe, just maybe, living together will prove he's different in all the right ways.

"Okay."

Before the word can leave my mouth, Barney's lips find mine. He doesn't plunder. His lips are feather soft on mine. "You won't regret it."

I don't have many regrets, but I know if I didn't take this chance, it would be one of the few things in my life I did regret. Time to dive in.

Chapter 33

Forget about the butterflies. When I'm with you, I feel the whole zoo.

"I don't want you to go," Barney says as he watches me put my earrings in.

I grunt. We've been having this argument all the damn day long. It's Saturday, three days since the accident, but he's acting like I got home from the hospital an hour ago. Tonight is Faith's bachelorette party, and I am not missing it. It's going to be absolutely spectacular. Of course, it is. I arranged everything.

"Love you, dude, but I am not missing this party."

I bend down to grab my shoes and I'm tackled from behind before being thrown on the bed. I bounce, but before I can catch my breath, Barney lands on top of me.

I shove his shoulders. "What are you doing? I'm going to be late."

"What did you say?"

"I said, I am going to be late," I enunciate my words like I'm speaking to a toddler.

"No, before that."

I think back. "I told you I'm not missing this party."

He taps my forehead with his fingers. "No, honey. What you said before that?"

"I didn't—" My mouth falls open and words desert me when I remember what I said. I've spent three days racking my brain for an idea on how to tell Barney the romantic I love him, and I let the words spill out in a moment of frustration.

He leans his forehead against mine. "Say them

again, please," he begs.

I sigh. I might as well get this over with. "I love you, you big oaf."

His eyes light up before they fall closed. "Thank you, honey. I will never abuse your love. You have my word."

I believe him. Am I scared out of my mind about taking the jump with him? I sure as hell am. Do I think he'll catch me when I fall? I do. I might be out of my mind, but I do.

"Now, get off of me. I need to leave, or I'll be late."

"Oh, you're going to be late, you can count on it." His lips meet mine and suddenly I don't give a rat's ass about punctuality.

I arrive at Faith's apartment fifteen minutes late and with an escort.

"I don't need a chaperone. I'm an adult in case you forgot," I grumble to Barney as we climb the stairs to her place.

"I didn't forget. Trust me, I was the one enjoying your very adult mouth not fifteen minutes ago."

The door's open when we arrive at the landing. Everyone in the room is gaping at us in silence as they watch us enter.

"What? We're older, we're not dead yet." I'd be more explicit, but Ollie's here. I won't be accused of corrupting my godson.

"Someone check her ring finger," Suzie says from her position lounging on the sofa.

I wave my left hand for everyone's perusal. "No reason to check. Barney and I aren't engaged, and we never will be. I'm not the marrying kind."

Phoebe harrumphs. "We'll see about that. I have Valentine's Day."

Suzie elbows her. "You're not supposed to tell her what day you have."

"Why not?" Phoebe bats her eyelashes at me. "Maybe Val loves me and wants me to win the bet."

I bark out a laugh. "Why would I want you to win?"

"Because I never win any of the bets," she pouts.

"Cuz you suck," Hailey says.

I clap my hands to get everyone's attention. "As much as I'd love to sit here and discuss my sex life, we have reservations."

"Where are we going?" Faith asks. "And why did you tell us to wear comfortable clothing we can move in?" She motions to my outfit of jeans and a turtleneck. "I figured you'd reserve somewhere for us to drink cocktails we can't pronounce until I start blabbing all of Max's secrets."

Max growls. "No worries, big guy," I tell him. "We won't be prying all of your sexy secrets out of Faith." I pause. "Yet." He frowns at me, and I wink.

"Is everyone here?" I count heads. Seven. Perfect. "Let's go."

Lexi jiggles a set of keys at us. "I have Lenny's SUV. We can all fit in one car."

"Why do you have Lenny's keys?" Chrissie asks the question everyone else is thinking.

Lexi shrugs. "He offered."

"And when did he offer?" Suzie shouts. "When you were playing hide the fire-breathing dragon?"

Phoebe shivers. "Fire-breathing dragon? Sounds dangerous."

Before I can follow the women out the door, Barney tags my hand and pulls me to the side. "Be careful."

"Sorry. No can do. When you're hunting zombies, the word careful doesn't exist." I wink at him, peck his cheek, and saunter off before he has a chance to respond.

"Zombies?" he shouts at my back. I wave and keep on walking.

We pile into Lenny's enormous SUV. "Why does a single man need this big of a vehicle?"

"I find it's better not to ask," Lexi says.

I give her directions and climb into the back. "Where's my spot?" I ask when I note all the seats are taken.

"Front passenger seat." Faith points to it. "And no arguments. Barney made me swear on a stack of bibles, I wouldn't let anything happen to you."

I shrug and get comfortable in the front seat. This way maybe they won't detect where we're going until we're there. Lexi parks in the lot next to the house and everyone exits the vehicle.

"Where are we?"

I clap my hands to get everyone's attention. "Welcome to your evening entertainment." I pause for dramatic effect. "Are you ready to kill some zombies?"

Suzie's hand shoots in the air. "I'm ready. I've been waiting for the zombie apocalypse for years."

Hailey smacks her hand out of the air. "You do know zombies aren't real?"

Mary Ann giggles. "Have I mentioned how much I love hanging out with you ladies lately?"

Chrissie marches to the front of the group. "I'll be taking point." She points to Lexi. "She'll bring up the rear."

I clear my throat. "We're here to have fun. This isn't a tactical operation."

Her grin is positively wicked. "Are you saying a tactical operation isn't fun?"

"Your definition of fun is whacked," I tell her before motioning to the group. "Let's go. We have a time slot and I don't want to miss it."

"How mad is Grayson going to be when he finds out you're running around in a haunted house chasing zombies while you're pregnant?" Hailey asks Suzie.

Suzie glares at her. "He's not going to be mad,

because he's never going to find out."

"I asked when I made the reservation. This activity is perfectly safe for pregnant women."

We check in and are given a safety briefing before moving on to the next room to receive our equipment.

"Nope," Chrissie says and points to a different weapon. "I want that one."

"You do realize this is laser tag. The weapons aren't real. It's make-believe."

She smirks. "Next thing I know you'll be telling me monsters and zombies don't exist."

"Zombies exist," Suzie chimes in. "Just you wait and see. The zombie apocalypse is coming."

And here I thought my crazy matched Suzie's. I know monsters exist. After the week I've had, damn straight I know monsters exist. But zombies? They do not exist. I know this despite my love of zombie television shows. What? They're addictive. Not as good as vampire romances but still good.

We team up in groups of two to go through the haunted house. When I notice Suzie and Phoebe together, I shake my head. "I don't think two pregnant women should be together."

"But they'll slow everyone else down," Hailey whines. She nods to her partner, Mary Ann. "Only the strong will survive."

Before I can respond, Chrissie and Lexi rush off. They're a well-oiled machine as they creep down the hallway before taking turns and entering the next room.

The equipment guy moans. "I hate it when we get the military types."

"They're CIA, not military," Suzie whisper-shouts.

Phoebe smacks her on the back. "I don't think you're supposed to tell anyone."

Hailey pushes past them. "Mary Ann and I are next."

They rush off with Hailey in the lead.

Once Hailey and Mary Ann are out of sight, Suzie and Phoebe are up. Suzie skips down the hallway while Phoebe lags behind her.

"We better go," I tell Faith. "Suzie will probably befriend the monsters and zombies."

We hear a scream and rush down the hallway into the next room. Lights are flashing on and off making it difficult to make out what's happening.

"I think my water broke. Oh no, I'm having the baby. It's way too early," Suzie shouts from where she's laying on the floor. Phoebe's standing next to her biting her lip in worry.

Faith rushes over to her. "Are you experiencing any other symptoms of labor?"

"I can't remember the symptoms of labor!" Suzie shouts.

"Are you having contractions? Do you feel pain in your stomach or lower back?"

Suzie touches her stomach and back. "No."

Faith reaches out her hand. "I don't think you're in labor."

"But I felt wetness," Suzie says as Faith helps her to her feet.

"You probably peed your pants in fright when the zombie came out of the trap door."

Suzie smiles. "This place is awesome. Five stars. Scares the pee right out of you." She runs off to the next room without waiting for Phoebe who trudges after her.

"This is amazing!" I shout at Faith. She shakes her head at me, but there's a smile on her face.

"Let's kill some monsters!" I thrust my weapon into the air and a monster rushes out at me. Faith kills it before I have a chance to lower my weapon.

"Okay. Lesson learned. No more raising my weapon in victory until the end."

When we exit the house sometime later, the rest of the group is waiting on the porch for us. As soon as they notice us, I raise my arms in victory. "Who's ready to celebrate stopping the zombie apocalypse with some drinks?"

Chapter 34

What happened to the two vampires who went on their first date? It was love at first bite.

A bug lands on my forehead, and I swat it away.

"Ouch!"

I open one eye to find Barney frowning at me. Oops. Not a bug then.

"Sorry," I apologize before rolling over.

Before I can get comfortable again, the blankets are yanked off of me. I scramble for them, but I don't have a chance. I groan. "Why are you being mean? I was nice to you last night."

And by nice I mean I attacked him the minute I got home from the bachelorette party. I didn't know it was possible to rip the button off a pair of jeans. It's not as sexy as it sounds. I lost my balance and ended up using his jeans for leverage. Don't worry. As soon as I regained my balance, I took advantage of him being pantless.

Barney wraps an arm around my waist and drags me to the edge of the bed. "And I showed my appreciation to you last night."

My belly dips and my center tingles. He sure did. But then he slaps my ass.

"Hey! No spanking!" I shove him away. He doesn't let me get far.

"I have a surprise for you today."

I glance at him over my shoulder. "Why didn't you say so in the first place? I love surprises."

"I know." He releases me. "Get dressed. I'll bring in

your coffee."

"What should I wear?"

"Something warm."

My nose wrinkles. Something warm? What kind of surprise requires warm clothes? It's winter in Wisconsin. And it is a winter unlike anything I've ever seen before. There's ten feet of snow on the ground – slight exaggeration – and everything's frozen. And these people go about their business as if it's no big deal. Back home this type of weather would have the entire city shut down.

An hour later we're driving out of the city in his truck. I cradle a cup of coffee in my hands. Barney's got the heat on full blast, but I swear I can feel the cold wind whipping off Lake Michigan into the truck.

"What are we doing?" I ask.

"It's a surprise."

I roll my eyes. He's said those same three words about five gazillion times now. "I'm surprised. Now, tell me what we're doing."

He chuckles and squeezes my thigh.

"At least tell me where we're going."

"West Bend."

Fat lot of good the name of some town does me. "What's in West Bend?"

"Parks, restaurants, shops."

I stick my tongue out at him. "You're being deliberately obtuse."

He winks at me. "I didn't lie."

Try as I might for the forty-five-minute drive, Barney doesn't crack and tell me what we're doing. He does repeat the town name of West Bend several times, though, until I tell him exactly where he can shove it.

I perk up when we exit the highway. I'm anxious to find out why we drove forty-five minutes to end up in a small town, but he turns left away from the town at the end of the exit. My brow wrinkles as I survey the area to find nothing but a country lane. Why are we here?

"What are we doing here?" I ask when he drives into a car dealership and parks.

"I'm going to show you how much fun the snow can be."

"Are we going sledding?" When he shakes his head, I guess again. "Skiing. I've never been skiing. I've always wanted to try. Is it hard?"

"If you want to learn how to ski, I'll teach you. Not today, though."

"Oh, are we going snowboarding then?"

He chuckles. "No. And, by the way, you need mountains for skiing and snowboarding."

"Ice skating, then? I can roller skate, so I imagine ice skating wouldn't be too difficult."

"No ice skating."

I throw my hands up in the air. "I give up. What else can you possibly do outside to show me how much fun snow can be?"

He grins. "Snowmobiling."

I rub my hands together. "Oh, I've never been on a snowmobile before. I've been on a four-wheeler, though. I bet a snowmobile is more fun."

I open my door and jump out of the truck. I promptly slip on the ice and have to grab the door handle to keep myself from falling. New rule. No jumping from trucks in the middle of winter. There are a lot of rules if you live in cold weather.

Barney laughs as he grasps my hand and helps me to the front door of the dealership. "I don't own a snowmobile. I'm renting one for the day," he explains as we enter. "First, we need to get you an outfit."

"An outfit? They have clothes here?" This day is getting better and better.

"I mean a snowmobile suit and some boots."

I glance down at my brown sheepskin boots.

"What's wrong with these?"

"They're not warm enough."

"They feel pretty warm to me."

"Let me put it this way for you. Do you want them covered in snow and slush?"

I cringe. "No way. These are new."

"Thus, snowmobile boots."

Do they have stylish snowmobile boots? I'm about to find out. Five seconds later, I have my answer. Snowmobile boots are most definitely not stylish. I hold up a pair of black boots. The bottom is rubber and the top are some kind of synthetic material, which the label claims is waterproof. Apparently, waterproof and pretty do not belong in the same sentence.

"Wow." I blink my eyes at the price tag, but the price doesn't change. It's still nearly two hundred dollars. "I'm not paying this amount for a pair of ugly boots I'll never wear again."

Barney snatches the boots from me. "First of all, I'm buying. And secondly, you're going to want these boots when winter comes."

"When winter comes? It's January. It's already winter."

He smirks. "Just wait."

"There's a foot of snow on the ground and it's fifty-thousand degrees below zero outside. Tell me this is winter."

"Come on. Let's get you a snowmobile suit." Shit. His non-answer means winter's going to get worse.

"Please tell me the snowmobile suits are better than the boots." They aren't. I can see it from here. They're all puffy. Oh sure, they have some pretty colors, but a favorable cut to make my not skinny body appear skinny? Not on your life.

Barney hands me a pink suit. "Try this on. I'll handle the snowmobile."

He points me in the direction of the restrooms. Snowmobiling doesn't seem like a great adventure now. Not when it involves an ugly outfit.

I feel like a pink teddy bear when I exit the restroom in my pink snowsuit. I waddle – because you don't walk in a snowmobile suit – to the counter where Barney's signing some paperwork. He smiles when he notices me.

"You're adorable."

"You need glasses. I'm a bloated teddy bear who dumped Pepto-Bismol all over herself."

He chuckles before leading me outside to a snowmobile. I clap and jump up and down. This is going to be a blast. "I can't wait to try this baby out. How fast can it go?"

"Bad news," Barney says. "I'll be the driver today since you don't have a snowmobile safety certification."

I try to cross my arms over my chest, but the stupid suit constricts my movements. I settle for stomping my foot. "If you had told me what we were doing today, I could have gotten certified."

"I wanted to make sure you enjoy it first."

I glare at him. Damnit. His answer is good one. "Fine. You can drive. Today."

Barney places a helmet over my head. "We can talk to each other using the intercoms built into these helmets."

He puts on his helmet and straddles the snowmobile. Too bad he's wearing a bulky snowmobile suit now, too. I would love to observe his thigh muscles stretch as he straddles the machinery. Down girl. This is no time to be thinking sexy thoughts.

Barney pats the seat behind him, and I climb on. "Wrap your arms around me."

Gladly. I scoot closer until his ass is nestled against my center and wrap my arms around him. Huh. Maybe now is the time to be thinking sexy thoughts after all.

He revs the engine and off we go. "There's a twenty-five-mile trail through the Kettle Moraine State Forest. I thought we'd drive up to Eden and have lunch there."

I tell him his idea sounds good despite having no idea where Eden is or what the Kettle Moraine State Forest is. He drives slow until we get on the trail. The trail isn't what I was expecting. It's a wide groomed path.

"Can't this thing go any faster? I feel like I'm in the back seat of Grandma Jo's car going to church."

I have no Grandma Jo as far as I know, but my words get Barney to speed up until the trees are whooshing by.

"Whoo hoo!" I shout and throw my hands into the air. He immediately slows down.

"Hold on or I'll show you just how slow Grandpa Jo can drive."

My arms drop and I hug his back. Once I'm settled, he speeds up again.

"Being safe is fun, too."

"Whatever," I mutter, but he's not wrong. Flying down the trail over the snow is fun. Don't tell Barney I said so.

By the time we reach the end of the trail, the cold is hitting me despite my Pepto-Bismol suit. I'm relieved when Barney drives into a parking lot and parks with the other snowmobiles in the snowmobile parking lot. Yes, there's a parking lot for snowmobiles.

"Let's get you warmed up with a hot buttered bourbon."

Hot buttered bourbon? I'm in.

Chapter 35

I want to spend the rest of my life trying to get out of debt with you.

"You ready?" Barney shouts into the bathroom.

I'm putting on the last touches of my going out make-up. It's the Friday night before Valentine's Day and when I returned home from work, Barney told me to get changed because we're going out. He didn't need to tell me twice.

We've been living together for a month now, and thus far, Barney hasn't transformed into a two-headed, four-armed monster. He's still the sweet man who brings me coffee in bed every morning and loves to surprise me with little gifts of flowers and chocolates. I'm starting to believe he isn't going to change. Scary. I know.

And work has been great for the past month, too. I thought I'd be out of a job once Mr. Davenport was arrested but another lawyer at the firm needed a legal secretary as her's is on maternity leave. Lucky for me, Mrs. Hall is the polar opposite of Davenport. She lets me call her by her first name, Anne, and gets her own coffee. She'll even bring me a special coffee from the place down the street when she returns from meetings. Is it wrong to hope her legal secretary decides to be a stay-at-home mom?

"I'm ready," I announce as I exit the bathroom.

Barney's eyes heat when he gets a look at my outfit. I smirk. "You like?" I twirl around to show him the back of the dress. Or rather, the lack of the back.

"Are you planning to torture me with your outfit all

night?"

I wiggle my eyebrows. "Not all night." He holds up a blindfold. "Mr. Lewis, you dirty old man, you."

"Will you wear it?"

"Are you going to tie me to the bed, too?"

The heat in his eyes explodes. "Do you want me to tie you to the bed?"

I've never been interested in being tied up, but the way Barney's looking at me with fire in his eyes has me reconsidering my position. "Maybe?"

"We'll table the matter until you're sure."

And yet another reason why I love this man. He's happy to push my boundaries, but only if he's confident I'm ready.

He swings the blindfold in his hand. "Will you wear this? I have a surprise for you."

"Does this surprise include me wearing the Pepto-Bismol suit?"

He chuckles. "It does not. Unless you want to."

"I most certainly do not."

I spin around and he places the blindfold over my eyes before tying it in the back. "It's not too tight, is it?"

"That's what she said!"

"Corny," he mutters.

"You're only saying that because I said it first." Barney thinks he's the master of corny dirty jokes.

He helps me into my coat and out the door and down to the truck. "You could have blindfolded me in the truck," I tell him once I'm settled and we're on the road.

"And miss watching you walk around with a blindfold on?"

"You're a horndog," I grumble despite how much I enjoy his horndog ways.

Time is weird when you're blindfolded. I have no idea how long we're driving when Barney parks and announces, "We're here." For all I know, we're in Chicago.

"This better not be the moment you decide to tell me you're an axe murderer and I have to run for my life. It will ruin my shoes."

"Ruin your shoes? If I'm an axe murderer, you have more important things to worry about than your shoes."

I gasp. "Take it back, mister. There's nothing more important than my shoes. Have you seen my shoes?"

I lift my leg to show him my strappy heels. The straps wrap around my ankles and continue up to my knees. This is our first Valentine's Day. I went all out. And, yes, I know Valentine's Day is technically tomorrow, but we have Faith's wedding tomorrow. A wedding doesn't count as a date unless it's your wedding and everyone knows I'm not the marrying kind.

My door opens and Barney lifts me out of the truck and into his arms. I don't bother telling him I can walk. I may be an independent woman, but I know when to keep my mouth shut. And the moment your man decides to carry you somewhere for a mysterious date is the time to shut it.

He sets me down. "Are you ready?"

"Beyond ready."

He unties my blindfold. "Ta-da."

I blink my eyes until they adjust to the light outside. I study my surroundings. We're standing on the sidewalk in front of an adorable craftsman house. It has a large porch on which hangs a porch swing. It's a-freaking-dorable.

"What are we doing here?"

"It's for sale. I thought we'd check it out since you don't want to live in the loft forever."

"We can check it out, but there's no way I can afford this place."

"No harm in looking."

He unlocks the front door and ushers me inside. My mouth drops open when I get a peek at the interior. It's gorgeous. No, not gorgeous. What's better than gorgeous? Sublime maybe.

The entire first floor is one big room with a staircase in the middle to separate the spaces. There's a kitchen at the back with a dining room next to it. In front, there are two living spaces on each side of the staircase. One has a large picture window while there's a fireplace in the other. There's no furniture except for a dining room table, but I can picture it with comfy sofas and chairs.

"There are four bedrooms and two bathrooms upstairs. Why don't you check them out?"

"Why would we need four bedrooms?"

"Our bedroom, a guest bedroom, a craft room for you, and an office for me."

He was awful quick with an answer. "Got it all worked out, haven't you?"

He places his hands on my shoulders and pushes me toward the stairs. "Go. Look around. I want to hear what you think of the place."

I sigh. "I'll look around, but I'm telling you now we can't buy this place. It's too expensive."

I climb the stairs anyway. House porn is my second favorite type of porn after all. The first room I peek into is small but workable as an office. The second and third rooms are identical. Slightly larger with decent sized closets.

I open the door to the last bedroom and gasp. It's not merely huge but it has a fireplace and a window seat. I could sit there and read or sew for hours. I open the door to the closet and nearly cry when I note the amount of space. There are tons of drawers and racks for hanging clothes. Plus, there's a shoe rack along the back wall. There's even a chaise lounge in the middle of the room.

The bathroom is next, and it doesn't disappoint. There's a soaking tub set in front of a large window. I imagine laying in the bath staring out over the wooded backyard. The vanity has double sinks, and there's a toilet in a separate room. And everything – the floors, the walls, the vanity – is marble.

Barney's waiting at the bottom of the stairs for me. "What do you think?"

"I love it and I'm mad at you."

He rears back. "Mad at me? Why are you mad at me?"

I poke him in the chest. "Because you showed me a gorgeous house, made me fall in love with it, and we can't afford it."

He captures my hand and places it against his heart. "Yes, we can."

I tug on my hand, but he won't let go. "No, we can't. *You* can afford it, but *we* cannot."

"All I have is yours."

"You're crazy."

He grins. "Crazy in love with you." He flips my hand over and drops a set of keys in it. "Happy Valentine's Day."

My heart races, and I feel sweat form on my brow. "Tell me you didn't buy this house."

He smirks. "I can't because I did buy this house."

"You don't buy houses for Valentine's Day. You buy flowers and chocolate. Take a girl out for a nice dinner."

"We'll do that as well." He motions to the dining room table, which is now set. There are lit candles in the center next to a large bouquet of red roses and a glass of champagne.

"Barney, I love you, but I can't afford this house. I'm being serious."

He cradles my face with his hands. "And I'm serious. All I have is yours. If you weren't opposed to getting married, we'd be married by now and it would be official. But I'm never going to force you to get married. I did the next best thing I could. I bought you this house."

"Whoa. Hold up. You bought *me* this house?"

He grabs my hand and leads me to the dining room table. "It's a done deal. No take-backs."

I inhale a deep breath and let it out. It doesn't help. This is all still crazy pants.

"Let's eat while it's hot." He pulls out a chair for me.

"Fine," I grunt as I sit down. "But I reserve the right to return to the buying the house business." At his nod, I ask, "What are we eating?" I don't wait for his reply before lifting the cloche off the plate. When I see the box on my plate, I jump to my feet. "You said you wouldn't force me to marry you."

"And I'm not." He picks up the box and flicks it open. And, because I'm a girl who loves jewelry more than she can afford to, I step close and peek inside.

Barney removes the sapphire ring from the box. It's beautiful. The sapphire is centered on a platinum ring with two diamonds nestled next to it.

"Sapphire?" I didn't expect a diamond but why sapphire?

"It reminds me of your eyes." He smiles at me. "I've never seen eyes as blue as yours. They sparkle when you're happy. And when I kiss you, the color darkens until it's nearly black."

He holds the ring out to me. "Will you be my valentine?"

"Will you stop buying me stuff like houses?"

"Never. I love spoiling you. Someone needs to make up for all the years you weren't taken care of, and I'm happy to fill the position."

Damnit. Why does he have a good answer for everything?

"I love you, Valerie Cook. You're it for me. The woman I didn't realize I've been searching for these last three decades. You erased all my pain I've been carrying around from Ruby's death and made me realize I'm not to blame."

"Of course, you aren't to blame. Don't be silly."

"I know buying this house is over the top, but I've seen the research history on your computer. I knew you'd love it and I know you've always wanted a home. A real home with a yard. I will always work my ass off to give you what you want."

Who am I to fight the man I love when he wants to give me the world? I slip the ring on my finger. "What if what I want is to skip dinner and show you how much I love you?"

His smile stretches from ear to ear. "Then, I'd say it's a good thing I had a bed delivered to the house today."

"Race you!" I spin around but I don't make it to the stairs before he catches me and throws me over his shoulder.

"I have the blindfold, too," he growls into my ear and goosebumps explode across my skin.

"Happy Valentine's Day to me."

Chapter 36

Do you play soccer? Because you're a keeper.

I'm bubbling with happiness as we enter McGraw's Pub the next day. I'm beyond excited Faith is getting her happily ever after with Max. She deserves it especially after what Silas put her through. The jerk.

The door opens, and I freeze on the landing. This doesn't resemble the pub. There are flowers everywhere, and the place is lit up with candles. The chairs are covered with white slipcovers with red bows tied around them. On the stage where the band plays there's now a wedding arch draped in red material.

"Who did all this?"

"It was Phoebe," Suzie says as she joins us. "She's our—" Her words cut off, and she screams. "Who had Valentine's Day?"

"This is my cue to leave." Barney kisses my hair before strolling off.

Hailey, Phoebe, and Mary Ann hurry over. Chrissie and Lexi follow them. They're too cool to hurry, though. They saunter over as if they have all the time in the world.

"I did," Faith shouts as she rushes out of the hallway in her wedding dress.

"What are you doing? Your groom can't see you in your dress before the wedding." I herd her backward toward the hallway.

She flashes her left hand in my face. "You mean husband."

"What?" I scream and grab her hand to study her

221

ring. "When did you get married? Why wasn't I invited?"

She blushes. "We had to get married for Max to adopt Oliver, and Max wasn't waiting until now to adopt my son." She sniffs. "He couldn't wait a month to adopt my son, Val. What did I ever do to deserve him?"

I blink fast to stop the tears welling in my eyes from falling. "If there's anyone who deserves the kind of man Max is, it's you."

She squeezes my hands and we stare at each other with tears in our eyes. Who would have thought this moment would ever occur? I couldn't have imagined it when I held her in my arms while she cried her eyes out after finding out Silas took yet another woman to her bed.

She lifts my hand and her eyes widen at the ring. "It's true! Barney and Val are engaged. I'm finally going to win a bet."

Hailey shoves her out of the way. "I had Valentine's Day. Not you. You wanted tomorrow."

I clap my hands. "Children. No one's a winner today."

Faith fists her hands on her hips. "Do not tell me you got engaged last week and didn't tell me."

"I'm not engaged."

Her shoulders sag. "Still afraid of marriage, then?"

"Just because I didn't drink the Kool-Aid doesn't mean I'm a scaredy cat."

"I drank the Kool-Aid," Suzie shouts. "It's delicious." She licks her lips as she ogles Grayson strutting toward us.

"Damn straight it is," Chrissie agrees as she stares at Wally who winks at her in return.

Mary Ann frowns. "It's deceiving."

"Woman! I told you you'll get your Valentine's Day present tonight," Sid shouts from across the room.

"You know he forgot this morning, and he's saying that to make it sound like he didn't," she mutters.

A Valentine for Valerie

"But forgetting means jewelry," Lexi points out.

"Good point."

"Are we having a wedding today?" Max asks as he claims Faith.

"What are you doing?" Faith's dad booms his question as he enters the pub.

"No telling anyone we're already married," Faith whispers before rushing to her parents.

The preacher taps on the microphone. "If everyone would take their seats."

"Is that the preacher who married you?" I ask Chrissie.

She nods. "We should probably have him on retainer. After your wedding, Lexi and Lenny are up."

"Not it!" Lexi and I shout at the same time.

"I've got Memorial Day," Chrissie says before leaving to find her seat.

"She's going to lose that bet." I cock an eyebrow at Lexi's response. "The man is in the friend zone and in the friend zone is where he'll stay."

I don't bother telling her I thought the same thing. It'll be more fun to watch her figure things out for herself. "I've got July fourth," I say instead and watch as her nostrils flare. Told you. Fun.

Barney throws his arm over my shoulders. "Are you getting into trouble, Trouble?"

We sit down in the front row next to a teenage girl. "Who's she?"

"It's Ollie's date."

I wave at her. "I'm Val."

"Bridget," she says.

There's no more time to talk as the wedding march begins, and we stand to watch Faith walk down the aisle. She's walking too fast to keep time to the music. Her dad, Martin, is struggling to keep up. He clamps a hand over her hand on his elbow to slow her down. Max laughs before jumping off the stage and meeting them in the middle.

"Pay up, losers," Wally says.

Barney mutters a curse before removing a twenty from his wallet and slapping it in Wally's outstretched hand.

Max tries to steal Faith away from her father, but Martin isn't letting go. Max frowns before offering Faith his elbow. She threads her arm through it and the three of them walk down the aisle together with Faith in the middle of her dad and her husband.

"Who gives this woman away to be married?" the preacher asks when they reach the stage.

"I do," Martin says and kisses Faith's cheek. He doesn't move away, though.

"I promise you, Martin. I've got her. I will love and cherish her until my last breath on this earth and thereafter."

"For goodness sakes, Martin. You know they're already married," his wife, Cora, shouts.

Faith gasps. "You're not supposed to know."

"A mother always knows."

"I'm sorry. I was going to tell you after today."

Cora waves her hand in dismissal. "My darling girl, I'm not mad. I'm glad you found a good one this time."

The preacher clears his throat. "If we could begin. Valentine's Day is a busy day for me."

Max cocks his eyebrow at Martin who grunts before moving away to sit next to his wife. Max hops onto the stage before helping Faith up.

"We are gathered together here to unite Max and Faith in marriage." He frowns. "Although it now appears the two are already married." He purses his lips before beginning his standard spiel. "This contract is not to be entered into lightly, but thoughtfully and seriously with a deep realization of its obligations and responsibilities. Please remember that love, loyalty, and understanding are the foundations of a happy and enduring home."

He gives Max and Faith a stern look before saying, "I understand you wrote your own vows."

Faith's eyes widen. "I didn't write my own vows. You never said anything about vows."

"There's my little spitfire."

"I'll show you my spitfire."

Max palms her neck before leaning his forehead against hers. "Darling, I don't care what you say during your vows." His voice lowers until it's too soft for anyone besides Faith to hear. Guessing by the blush blossoming on Faith's face, his words are not for the general population.

He kisses her forehead before straightening and taking her hands. "I'm ready," he tells the preacher.

"By all means. Proceed." I know one preacher who isn't getting a tip today.

"Faith McGraw." He winks. "I vow to be grateful for every day I share with you. Not every day will be easy. Some will be a complete shit show. But, at the end of the day, I'll be here. I will always love and appreciate you for all the days of my life."

Faith holds out her palm and Ollie walks forward to drop a ring in her hand. She places the ring on Max's finger. "Max McGraw, I vow to love you no matter how stubborn you are. I vow not to kick your butt when you refuse to realize you're wrong and I'm right. And I vow to be a soft place for you to land on those shit show days."

"By the authority vested in me by the State of Wisconsin, I now pronounce you husband and wife."

Max's head descends and he kisses Faith. He lingers until Lenny wolf whistles. When he comes up for air, the preacher clears his throat.

"You may now kiss the bride."

Max ignores the preacher's sarcasm. "Don't mind if I do."

Ollie feigns gagging. "I mind."

Phoebe raises her hand. "I'm with the kid."

Hailey shoves her. "You need to get over your obsession with Pops kissing Faith. They're married. Kissing is going to happen. Probably, a lot."

I wiggle my eyebrows at Barney. "We don't need to be married to kiss."

"We sure don't."

His lips find mine, and I cling to his suit lapels. He tastes of the outdoors, beer, and something unique to Barney. I call it Eau de Barney.

"That's not going to happen," Lexi shouts and I lift my head to investigate what's happening.

Lenny has Lexi pinned to her seat. He growls. "It is."

"Dream on." She pushes him out of her way, stands, and walks away. Lenny watches her, but I keep my eyes peeled to him. He's not hiding the longing he's feeling.

"This is going to be fun."

"It sure is, honey. It sure is," Barney says with a wink.

I don't think he's talking about Lenny and Lexi. But the idea he's talking about us and our life together doesn't cause panic anymore. Not even a tiny twinge of doubt. How can I possibly doubt this man when he kept me safe, watched over me when I was injured, and bought me a freaking house?

"I love you." Those three words don't hold me hostage anymore.

"Until my dying breath," he whispers before his lips find mine again.

About the Author

D.E. Haggerty is an American who has spent the majority of her adult life abroad. She has lived in Istanbul, various places throughout Germany, and currently finds herself in The Hague. She has been a military policewoman, a lawyer, a B&B owner/operator and now a writer.

Made in the USA
Coppell, TX
29 November 2022